SYNTHESIS

SYNTHESIS

A collection of 27 short science fiction stories from around the globe

First Published 2016 by Fantastic Books Publishing

Cover design by Heather Murphy
Cover art by Alvaro Escudero

ISBN: 9781-909163-98-0

DEDICATION

To my Grandmother Margaret Kot who 31 years ago put the dream of this anthology into motion by handing my 8 year old self a copy of Ray Bradbury's short science fiction collection 'the Golden Apples of the Sun'.

Thanks Granny.

ACKNOWLEDGEMENTS

With thanks to the authors. You have my eternal gratitude for contributing your work to this collection.

FOREWORD BY ROBERT LLEWELLYN

Apart from the simple joy of allowing the human imagination run free, science fiction writers can also reflect our current situation with startling clarity. The genre allows the writer to experiment with ways human beings can either live in harmony or survive challenges we can barely comprehend, they can be the modern equivalent of fairy stories or parables, morality tales and thought experiments.

Reading science fiction (as opposed to watching sci-fi movies) also allows us to create our own vision of the world the writer describes.

I'm not saying reading is better than watching, obviously there are some magnificent examples of sci-fi on the small screen coming to Dave in the UK later this year, but it is a different experience.

So delve into Synthesis, there's bound to be a story or two that will expand your mind.

Robert

NOTE FROM THE PUBLISHER

Hello dear reader,

I'm Dan from Fantastic Books Publishing, the publisher behind this collection, and I wanted to tell you how it came about.

My dream since my Grandmother first put a copy of Ray Bradbury's short science fiction collection 'The Golden Apples of the Sun' in my hand at age 8 has always been to someday release an equivalent collection of thoughtful, exciting and well written short science fiction. Now, at age 39, it has finally happened.

The wonderful team here at Fantatsic Books Publishing has worked hard to produce an homage to the classic science fiction collections of the 40s and 50s. I can't thank the authors and editorial team enough.

Spanish digital artist Alvaro Escudero and cover designer Heather Murphy have created a cover of which I am immensely proud and I thank them from the bottom of my heart.

The authors themselves have written some of the most amazing short science fiction stories I have ever read and, alongside their professional counterparts, have helped to produce this eclectic and thought provoking collection.

Between you all, you have made a small independent publisher very happy.

Thank you.

Dan Grubb
CEO
Fantastic Books Publishing

Contents

A Cosmic Dilemma

by Boris Glikman

It is the middle of a fresh December day.

I'm alone in the front yard, building a snowman, when the whole Universe lands beside me.

I can see myriads of stars, galaxies, clusters and superclusters whirling inside it. The blackness of its oceans of emptiness contrasts sharply with the whiteness of the snow.

The cracked magnifying glass and the frayed tape-measure that I always carry with me, being the budding scientist that I am, have awaited this day.

I examine the Universe, trying to solve that age-old vexing question of whether it is infinite or not. I search for a maker's label listing the Universe's specifications: dates of manufacture and expiration, gross and net weights, its exact ingredients, but alas, the tag is nowhere to be found.

The Cosmos looks stretched, too oblong for my liking, so I pick it up and mould it into a nice spherical shape.

It then occurs to me that, out of all the people in the world, the Universe has chosen to land at my feet. This must surely be, and I don't think I'm being too presumptuous in arriving at this conclusion, a sign of some significance and a personal message, the meaning of which, while not as yet entirely clear, is undoubtedly an auspicious one, although the method of communication is rather dramatic and not very subtle at that.

But then a devastating thought: what if this is the result of a wish made for a Christmas gift

A few weeks ago. I cannot lie to myself and deny that, in a moment of frivolous avarice, I wished for the entire world. I dread the punishment I will surely receive from my parents for making the Universe fall from the sky, the evidence of which will be harder to hide than that broken vase.

I trudge home, burdened by the consequences of my actions and not being able to see a way out of the situation. Once in my room, I throw myself on to my bed and immediately fall into a deep sleep. I awake after only a few hours, feeling quite refreshed, and take a quick shower.

There's a commotion outside and so I run down the stairs, quickly and excitedly, with my neighbours following me.

A white hole has fallen down into the communal backyard. There it is, lying on the ground. The unearthly hue of its whiteness, infinitely purer than the colour of the fresh snow it has landed in, captivates me.

I cannot resist entering it, even though I know that I am breaking every law of physics by doing so. To my disappointment, nothing unusual happens when I exit through the other side and walk away from it.

I am almost happy to see the white hole rise up to the sky, according to the Universal Law of Levitation that we learned about in school, for I had hoped that it would take me to a place where I could escape from the horrible predicament I've gotten myself into and start things anew, yet it had brought me only disillusionment.

My neighbours run back to the apartment block and I follow them dejectedly, looking over my shoulder to make sure that I don't bump into them. Once back in my flat, I dry myself thoroughly from the shower that I am about to have and then lie down in bed, feeling well rested from the deep sleep that I now fall into.

BORIS GLIKMAN is a writer, poet and philosopher from Melbourne. His stories, poems and non-fiction articles have been published in various publications, as well as being featured on national radio. https://bozlich.wordpress.com/ This is the first of three of his stories in this collection.

Alice

by David Styles

Alice looked across the field of wheat she had planted a few months ago. The crop would soon be ready to be harvested. Sowing the seeds had been hard work, nurturing the plants had been tedious, and harvesting would be back-breaking. But it was work that she could do; and do well. Alice took satisfaction from knowing that she was fulfilling her role in her community. Like so many before her, Alice felt justifiably pleased with herself for a job well done.

In this new world order people took pride in their labours.

Black clouds were hanging in the distance. She knew that those clouds meant rain when they were overhead; but they were a long way away, and were heading elsewhere. If there was any justice in this world they would go down to the mill and rain on Joshua the Miller. It wasn't so much because she disliked Joshua; more that it annoyed her that no one else could see how lazy and manipulative he was.

Many people told her that Joshua was cantankerous and set in his ways because he was an old man, and that she should be patient with him. Alice however knew better. Joshua didn't like her. He didn't like the fact that she refused to get confused when he tried to cheat her like he cheated everyone else.

And so his sarcastic tongue would lash out at her more than at anyone else. The simple fact that Alice, like Joshua, could count her worth annoyed him. Alice could add and subtract, multiply and with a little effort divide. And she could read and write, albeit not fluently. Nevertheless that was a rare talent these days.

She therefore knew when Joshua was short-changing her and everyone else in the community. Which was most of the time.

Alice wondered how the others managed. Obviously they were easy prey. Not just cheated out of what was rightfully theirs, but also cajoled and shamed into doing all sorts of work that was not theirs to do. Very few of them understood Joshua's written tallies that were viewed with reverence by the gullible; and Joshua was not above taking advantage of the deference that ignorance shows to understanding.

Alice had long suspected that Joshua did far less than his fair share of the work in the village by shaming and tricking others into doing it for him. 'Don't you remember.' He would kindly smile. 'I gave you that linen only last month,' or 'I stood a double turn at fire-watch only last week.' As evidence he would produce his ledgers and records; paperwork that was comprehensible to an increasingly small minority these days.

The majority would smile and nod, ashamed to admit that they had no idea of the significance of Joshua's squiggles on those pages. And so they would take Joshua's turn at watching the flocks, or moving the rubbish, or fetching firewood with a proud feeling that it was their duty. No one but Alice ever saw the smug smile on Joshua's face as he put his feet up. How could they; he'd tricked them into doing his jobs.

She sometimes wondered what annoyed her most – Joshua's dishonesty or everyone else's being tricked by it. Both Paul who grew the potatoes and Diane who milked the herds had been fooled by Joshua so many times, but they seemed to make it through the winters just as she did. Even if they did carry Joshua with them.

Occasionally she wondered if she could convince everyone else that they were being cheated by teaching them numbers, showing them reading and writing. Alice had a vague sense that sharing her knowledge would be

6

the right thing to do, but she didn't really know how to go about it. She could teach planting, hoeing, tilling, harvesting. Showing and sharing something practical was easy. But conveying something abstract wasn't.

She'd once tried teaching what she knew to Oliver, but realised that she didn't understand any of it. She knew what to do with the numbers and how to form and say the letters, but the 'why' eluded her.

She'd learned what she knew from her grandmother, a wizened woman old before her years, who kept apologizing to Alice for not being a proper teacher. Apparently when grandmother was a girl she'd been to class, and had seven other children as playmates. Grandmother also claimed that her grandmother had been in a class with thirty other children. And that there had been over ten similar classes in what was called a school.

Alice had done the sums. Three hundred people. She didn't believe it. That was about the number of people in the whole world, wasn't it? She'd done this head-count many times.

There were twenty-two of them in the community that lived and worked together in and around the Great Harbour. Alice knew of eleven people who would periodically come up and down the old road with wagons burdened with all sorts of things which they would trade for what had arrived on the ships.

There were nineteen more brave souls (including Oliver) who came and went with the four ships that regularly sailed in and out of the Great Harbour. Oliver had told her of the villages across the sea – his ship would variously sail to seven other such places which were slightly bigger or smaller than their collective at the Great Harbour.

Oh – she nearly forgot to count the dozen or so people along the coast at Folk's Town. She always forgot them.

Occasionally, maybe once a year, a ship would arrive unannounced in the Great Harbour carrying strangers. Once such a ship arrived with a crew of ten.

Alice could account for about three hundred people. That was a lot.

She roused herself from her reverie. From her vantage point in the sloping wheat field at the top of the cliffs Alice could see the Great Harbour below. She looked across the sea. There was a speck on the horizon that had noticeably grown larger this last hour. A ship on its way back from Calay or Rotten Dam?

She looked beyond the ship. Alice knew that the low clouds across the sea that were only visible on very clear days weren't low clouds at all. They were another place just like hers. With fields of crops to grow and flocks and herds to tend. She found it hard to believe, but it had to be true; ships left the Great Harbour heading to those horizons laden with cargo, and would return days later laden with different cargo. At night she had even once seen the lights of far Calay.

One of those ships was clearly on the way home now. It would be a few hours before it got to the Great Harbour, but Alice would be waiting for it. Helping unload was something that everyone did. Everyone helped if they could. Generations long dead would have described it as a civic duty, but Alice liked unloading the ships. Tending the wheat fields could be rather dull, even if everyone openly acknowledged that was her forte. And whilst helping unload the ship she would get to see Oliver. If that was his ship.

Oliver sailed the waters between the Great Harbour and the far horizon, and had done so for more than fifteen summers. He and Alice had played together as children; even though he was six summers older. And with the passing years they had become more than friends. If only he wasn't away for so long. Alice often wished she had chosen someone other than a sailor, but with so few people in this world one could not be too fussy about one's choice of partner.

It was he who had first told her about the lands across the seas, but on seeing her incredulity all those years ago he had quickly changed the subject of their conversation. The younger Alice's world was very small. But over the years Oliver had occasionally mentioned the lands of 'Felix's Toe' and 'Boloyn', and she knew he saw it as one of his major victories in life that he had eventually convinced Alice that these places were real.

Alice was waiting on the dockside when the ship came in. She wasn't alone – over half of the people who made up their community were there; ready to unload the cargo, to fetch and to carry, As were two travelling merchants of Alice's acquaintance whose carts they would load with whatever had come in from over the seas.

As the ship docked, everyone set to their tasks. They had all done this before, so many times. There was no need for direction; no need for a leader. The ship was soon unloaded, the waiting wagons filled. Usually after an unloading people would drift away in small groups, but this afternoon something was different. Alice had sensed it as she'd greeted Oliver, as they kissed, as they worked. Oliver had not been unfriendly or rude; far from it. But like the rest of the ship's crew he'd been distant, distracted. Others had noticed it too, and as the work finished it was Joshua, blunt as ever, who voiced what everyone was thinking. 'Well, what's the matter?' his gruff tone boomed out.

Oliver looked first at his feet, then at his fellow sailors. One of the more grizzled ones coughed and, seeing that all eyes were on him, started. 'Well … it's like this,' and then fell silent.

'Like what, Simon?' asked Joshua.

Simon was rather hesitant. He'd never spoken in front of such a crowd before. Oliver stepped in for him. 'Well …' He paused. 'It was odd. We went to Boloyn like we do every other week, but there was no one there. The harbour was empty.'

'Perhaps they were busy' ventured Potato Paul (he hated that name!)

'No' replied Oliver. 'There was no one there. They always see the ship coming and are ready to meet us. Like you were. We waited there for two days. No one came. We went looking. We couldn't find anyone.'

Alice sat through the silence that followed this revelation, as did everyone else. No one really knew what to say. Strange happenings in a place which she'd never visited (and likely never would) was a matter of indifference to her. She said so out loud, and soon regretted her words.

Joshua's tone was bitter. 'What use will your wheat be if we can't trade it for their hides and wines?' Alice hadn't thought of that.

Oliver was speaking again. 'We went up to Calay,' he repeated. 'They knew about Boloyn. They said they'd heard that the same had happened in other places.'

'Other places?' wondered Alice. And her mind spun as Oliver told her of Lavrer and Dyep which were now ghost towns as well. The people in Calay had heard tales of raiders. 'Raiders?' asked Alice.

'Yes, raiders!' snapped Joshua. 'They come, take what they want and go.'

Alice couldn't understand this at all. For all that her community had no rules and no leadership, everyone knew that you didn't take without giving. Otherwise no one would ever give to you again.

'Oh you silly girl!' swore Joshua. 'They don't ask before they take. They take. And if you have anything to say about the matter, they will take you as well ...' Joshua fell silent as he looked out to sea.

On the far horizon there were dark clouds, Very dark clouds. The smoke of burning Calay. And coming across the water directly at them was the largest fleet of ships anyone had ever seen.

DAVE STYLES – husband, father and grandfather. Biomedical scientist by trade, has been bitten by anacondas and tigers, and was voted "Kent Geocacher of the Year 2015". This is David's first of two stories in this collection.

Follow his life at:

http://mankybadger.blogspot.co.uk/

All in the mind

by John Hoggard

The five-second-long symphony of destruction began with the sharp explosion of fragmenting headlamp glass. A moment later there was a subtle hiss of superheated halogen gas escaping from its glass prison. With a crack JON50N shattered as the colour-coordinated bumper it was attached to folded up like paper.

The chorus, a scream of tortured metal, rose like a tidal wave over the early melodies. Howls of mercy as it was torn, stretched and crushed. It seemed to plead for understanding as the beautiful sleek curves it had grown accustomed to were wrenched into distorted shapes of horror and destruction.

Underneath this crashing, percussive roar were softer, more gentle sounds. A careful ear could pick out fuel, water and lubricant pipes rupturing and splitting, spraying their contents into the air like blood from a severed artery.

The heart of the car, devoid of this high octane life, shuddered and died as it was ripped from its mountings and thrown around the engine bay like a soft drink can in the autumn wind.

The final crescendo to this opening act was the explosive shattering of a windscreen. In the relative silence that followed, a deadly rain filled the air as its remnants peppered the tarmac and punctured flesh with stilettos of glass. And as the main symphony died away, leaving only the steady, but ever slowing, metronomic *tick, tick, tick* of a wheel spinning on a broken axle, there was a moment to reflect that there had been a second melody. It had been an organic air, the tune of breaking bones, tearing flesh and crushed internal organs. It had been the tune of Death overwhelming a mortal man's life and only in the suddenness of its ending was it possible to acknowledge that it had been there at all.

As wheel and heartbeat slowed in unison, the final, delicate sounds were of liquid dripping on to wet tarmac. A mixture of oil, petrol, blood and urine escaped from the carnage in rivulets of red and brown.

Open your eyes Doctor Johnson. Quickly please, we haven't much time.

Pardon? What?

Open your eyes!

Hey, I can't move.

Unimportant, open your eyes.

Unimportant? Unimportant! Don't you understand? I can't move!

OPEN YOUR EYES! Are your eyes open Doctor Johnson?

Yes.

What do you see?

Nothing.

Be more precise Doctor Johnson, it's important. What do you see?

I can't see anything.

Blackness?

No! NOTHING! Black is a colour and I can't even see that.

Excellent.

How can it be excellent? I'm blind.

You're not blind Doctor Johnson, this is the clearest you have ever seen. The clearest any human being has ever seen. Now Doctor Johnson tell us about the dream.

What dream?

THE DREAM. Tell us about the Device.

You mean the Free Motion Device? But that is just a dream, a childhood fantasy. I want it to work, but it can't.

Then you have nothing to lose. Tell us about the Device. Tell us everything about it. Tell us how it works, how to make it. We need to know.

It's just a box, a box in a dream. I've studied for degrees in physics, mathematics, chemistry and engineering and none of them have shown me how to build my FMD. They haven't even shown me where to start.

But you know where to start. You always have. You knew when you were just six years old.

The drawing of the plane?

Yes. See how easily it all comes back? Tell us about the plane.

I drew a plane, all windows and pointy wings and it had some stairs coming down from a door and all these people were going inside and my father looked over my shoulder and said that I had forgotten to draw the wheels, because the plane wasn't touching the ground. So I drew a little box inside the middle of the plane and my father asked me why I hadn't drawn any wheels and I told him it didn't need any wheels because of the box.

What type of box?

That's what my father asked. I told him it was a magic box. So he asked me where the box got its power to keep the plane in the air, and I told him.

Where?

Everywhere.

So what is in the box?

I don't know. I've spent my life trying to work it out. I've hidden myself away from the world for weeks at a time and I still never found the answer.

There were too many distractions, you could not focus properly.

What distractions? No TV, no radio, newspapers or telephones.

The effect the rising and setting sun had on your body, the need for sleep, the

13

beating of your heart, the rattle in your chest from a threatening infection. The room would be too hot, too cold. The movement of the air over your skin, an ignored bladder full of piss, an empty stomach needing sustenance.

I don't understand.

Life, Doctor Johnson. Life was your distraction, as it is for every human. Now what was in the box?

I don't know! I don't know what was in the box. I don't know where to start.

Can you tell us what isn't in the box? Can you start there?

Yes, I think so.

Tell us what isn't in the box.

The box has no moving parts. Moving parts waste energy. They produce friction, heat, noise, vibration. That's why the internal combustion engine is such a terrible device.

We know about internal combustion engines Doctor Johnson, We need to know about your device. Tell us what else isn't inside the box.

No electronic components, no method of collection, no method of transmission. All require energy, all bleed it unnecessarily from the whole. Even pushing an electron through a wire or moving a photon through a fibre optic needs energy. Too much energy. It must be free. The device must not react or interact it must simply be. Its existence must be everything, all that is required.

Good, good. Tell us more. Show us, Doctor Johnson, show us the box.

I can't.

You can Doctor Johnson and you must. Show us the box.

How?

It's already here, in your mind. We can sense it but only you can truly see it. Now concentrate Doctor Johnson. Concentrate.

Do you see it?

Oh yes. We see it. Now Doctor Johnson, show us what's inside the box.

I can't.

You can. Don't think about it. Your mind already knows, but your conscious must see it. We must see it. Stretch out your mind and enter the box.

Oh my god!

That's it! Relax Doctor Johnson, go deeper, into the structure.

These bondings can't be right. The composition of this material is impossible.

Not impossible, we're looking at it. Merely improbable, this is the start you could never find. Now, quickly Doctor Johnson, time is very short. Push beyond the quantum levels Doctor Johnson, beyond the fabric of Spacetime as you currently understand it, into the multi-dimensional. Go!

I can't believe it, it's, it's so … beautiful. So complicated and yet so simple. So many dimensions intertwined … It's not even a box, that's just how it manifests itself in these limited dimensions … I can't believe my thinking had been so unimaginative. It's … Hey, where'd it go? Wait, I want to see more. Please. Please. P—

Sorry Doctor Johnson. Goodbye.

WAS IT ENOUGH THEN? THE IMAGE WAS VERY BRIEF.

It was enough. The human race has proven potential and will remain relatively undisturbed, at least, while we're in a position to assure that is the case.

SHALL I CANCEL THE INVASION ORDERS?

Yes, best we not draw attention to this species just yet and those troops are better utilised elsewhere. Besides, we have the box now.

JOHNSON'S MAGIC BOX.

Yes, Johnson's Magic Box. The dream of a six-year-old human.

AMAZING.

Quite, but come now we have much work to do. We now know what to build but not yet how to build it. Let us hope we overcome that difficulty before we lose this war.

JOHN HOGGARD has been writing since at least the age of six, when a local newspaper printed one of his science-fiction stories. Buoyed by this early success he has been writing science-fiction ever since. This is the first of two stories John has in this collection.

Follow John on Twitter: @DaddyHoggy

Amerika in the Sky (in Memoriam)
by Boris Glikman

I remember that day starting off ordinarily enough; there I was playing in the open field not that far from home, the sky azure with hardly a cloud blighting its face.

I was alone as usual, for my mother didn't let me play with the other kids. I never really wanted to play with them anyway. I always knew I was different, I could see things that they could not and understood matters that they had no inkling of.

This disparity between my physical and mental development did cause me problems; there was always the inner conflict between the body's desire to be a child, carefree and frivolous, and the mind's desire to think deep thoughts, explore complexities and subtleties of the world, create abstruse theories.

That day the body scored a victory for there I was playing in the open field …

The lie of the land is so perfectly flat I can see unencumbered all the way to the horizon.

As the day proceeds, the heavens rotate slowly on their axis. Towards mid-morning something very odd catches my eye on the eastern horizon. It is something that I have never seen in the sky before but there it is before me, arising slowly from beneath the edge of the earth.

By some process, the continent of North America has become attached to the celestial sphere at the place where land and heavens meet and is slowly getting unravelled from the crust of the Earth.

America is now being carried along by the turning of the heavens.

I can clearly see its unmistakable shape and the features of the land: the whiteness of Alaska, the mighty rivers, the mountain chains, the major cities, the wheat fields, the pine forests, the Mojave Desert.

At first, while the continent is still at a shallow angle in the sky, the North American people seem to be enjoying their unique experience, smiling, laughing, some even waving to me down below.

As the heavens continue their inexorable turning and the continent slowly approaches the celestial zenith, the fun and the mirth turns to panic and despair.

At midday the continent reaches the highest point in the sky, hanging precisely upside down and the Sun is eclipsed. Some rays are still able to sneak around the frayed edges of the landmass, but the diffracted beams are of a different hue to natural sunlight and create an eerily muted illumination.

The view from down below looks like a disturbed anthill on a gigantic scale, with millions of Americ-ants scurrying frantically in random directions, trying to save their colony from some uncouth hooligan poking at it with a stick. If not for the desperate gravity of the situation, it would be almost comical to observe the way that they are trying to cope with the catastrophe that has befallen them.

But how does anyone deal with their world becoming upside down? All the survival instincts developed over the eons of evolution are now hopelessly irrelevant.

The people are now in their most precarious position, desperately trying to grab anything that is firmly rooted in the ground, from blades of grass, to soil itself. Even when they completely lose all grip on land, still they attempt to find some protuberance in the fabric of the sky that they can hold on to, to give themselves just one more instant of life.

Some of the people hold hands as they fall, others are kissing and hugging, while others still are engaged in more intimate activities. I look away, not wishing to intrude upon the privacy of their last significant moments together.

Even at this critical time, the teenagers cannot suppress their competitive streaks and are racing to determine who can fall the fastest and hit the ground first and hardest.

As if to make up for their lives being cut short, the falling people seem to age decades in the few instants of their descent.

I can see weddings taking place and then being consummated. I hear babies crying, I watch them grow, they'll learn secrets of the sky that I'll never know. Parents are teaching their children the facts of life, teaching them how to behave, how to tie their shoelaces. Boys are turning into adolescents, having their first shave and diffidently asking girls out for a first date.

I see friends shaking hands, saying 'how do you do', they're really saying 'goodbye to you' and I think to myself what a horrible world. I watch mothers whispering last words of love to their children, men writing their final wills and testaments, people coming to terms with their fate.

As the continent remains in the apex of the sky, buildings' foundations start to loosen, roots of plants are no longer able to cling to the soil; the once mighty rivers empty their banks in cataclysmic downpours of unprecedented proportions.

After all the signs of civilisation and life – buildings, forests, houses – disappear, the ground itself begins to give way and disintegrate. The earth slowly loses its compactness and adhesiveness, dripping down in small spurts at first and then in great lumps. Here and there, the liquid magma substratum is peeking through the locations where the entire continental crust has fallen off.

As the whole continent continues to break up, a colossal downpour of bodies, concrete, trees, mud, water, cars, houses, rock, soil all mixed up together into a terrible blend, threatens to engulf the world below and destroy our lives too.

Thankfully, some clouds appear and block these scenes of suffering and chaos, but then they disperse and again I'm unable to look away.

But what right do I have to look, God-like, upon the numberless agonies? Who am I, a small boy, to watch scenes of suffering so terrifying that even Death itself turns its bony face away in fright?

After an interminable span of time, the continent begins to move away from the zenith. The Sun re-appears in the sky, whole and wholesome, able to shine again. For a moment it seems to me that the sky is empty and blue, with its innocence intact, just the way it appeared early this morning. But morning happened a million irreparable lives ago, in that innocent era when things like this could not be envisaged.

A fortunate few have managed somehow to survive the nearly total destruction of the landscape of North America and they are approaching the horizon and security of the ground again. Thank goodness they now will be able to land safely and be lauded as heroes.

Alas, my hopes are proven to be woefully inaccurate. For when this ill-fated continent reaches the horizon again, it collides sharply with the unyielding ground that is already there. Two continents attempt to occupy the same location at the same time and one of them has to lose out.

Northern Canada and Alaska are the first to go. Bit by bit they are torn apart as the stationary earth refuses to shift and stands firm its ground. Those remaining alive, that I thought would be the lucky survivors, are crushed to dust. A horrible grinding noise is created that resounds across the span of the land, like a million fingernails scraping together across an inconceivably large blackboard.

I cannot help but rush to their aid, to try to save at least some lives. Suddenly I halt as I remember that the horizon is an illusory point in the distance that keeps receding further and further as you run towards it and so I would never be able to reach the doomed ones.

By now, more than half the continent has been ground into fine powder as the merciless process continues without ceasing. The major metropolises of the United States, the founts of so much knowledge, art, music, creative energy, are being pulverised into nothingness.

Icy pieces of Alaska intermingle with the glassy shards of New York City and with bits of tinsel of Los Angeles. Would it ever be possible to reconstruct America from these clouds of dust? Civilisations, cities, entire countries have been rebuilt from ruins before, but this is annihilation on a thoroughly unmitigated scale, from which there's surely no coming back.

'Well, there goes the New World,' I think wistfully. 'No longer will we have America in our lives, no more remains of that cultural centre of the world from which we get our TV programs. It is gone in the cruellest fashion, right before my eyes. And yet its ashes and dust will settle all over the world, infusing every cell of the remaining planet. Forever more, it will provide fertilisation for the world to go on growing and progressing the way America once did and we will be able to say proudly that we now all have a little bit of America in our very souls.'

Many years have passed since the day we lost America. For decades, the sky was stained red with the blood of the hapless victims, its mysterious beauty forever blighted by the destruction it had wrought upon the millions.

Death itself was not able to watch so much pain and carnage and was inconsolable, crying the rain down that day. It could not bring itself to accept what had happened and tried to refuse entry to the millions of new arrivals knocking on its door and asking to be let in, for it did not foresee their coming and strenuously denied playing any role in their demise.

Never before had so many died at the same time, in full view of the rest of humanity. Nothing would ever make the world regain its lost innocence and America, whose ceaseless creativity once brought the world so much entertainment and pleasure, now became the cause of humanity's greatest sorrow.

The world gasped, the world cried, the world mourned, and then it went on living. For a long time afterwards, all our activities down on earth seemed insignificant and frivolous by comparison with what transpired up above.

'Where was God while America was being destroyed? How could such a day

ever come to pass?' we wanted to know. Did God look the other way and ignore what went on that day? Or was God Himself paralysed with fear at what He witnessed and could do nothing to help the victims? Was this event such an unexpected aberration of the natural order of the universe that not even He foresaw it coming? Was this His will being done or was this done against His will?

Time itself stopped in the face of such tragedy and then tottered on uncertainly, in a punch-drunk manner, the way we staggered around in a daze down on Earth. And so we could not tell if days or years passed by, for Time trudged forward erratically, sometimes taking steps back, as it too tried to reverse the flow of the events and return to the innocent happiness of the past

Ships were forbidden from approaching the ugly scar that lay across what was once the New World. However, that didn't stop the morbid sightseers from making their way there to gawk at what became known as Ground Absolute Zero or taking chartered flights over what was once a mighty country, bustling with life

Every time that I look up, I see it all again: the chaos, the panic, the destruction, America writhing in its final death throes, a thousand lives being cut short with each passing minute.

In the end however, what I have written is only a crude and clumsy depiction. Words that I have used to convey what I saw and felt that day are now impotent, bloodless beings that have lost their vital life-force together with America. And so I will speak no more, except in that most authentic and most profound language of all – absolute silence.

BORIS GLIKMAN is a writer, poet and philosopher from Melbourne. His stories, poems and non-fiction articles have been published in various publications, as well as being featured on national radio. https://bozlich.wordpress.com/ This is the second of three of his stories in this collection.

Dying Star

by Marko Susimetsä

Fields of green spread in front of him, still in the deadly rays of the sun filtering through the dome above. The land once used to grow crops was now seized by weeds. But even so, it was a beautiful sight; gently rolling fields filled with life, tasting the natural light of the sun for the first time in their existence.

Carc smiled, though he was burdened with the knowledge that he was the last person ever to see it and that it was his responsibility to remember it as it had once been. With some reluctance, he looked up at the transparent dome and the sun that was to end it all. Even through the fifty metres of water, the sun was too bright to look at. Soon the ocean would no longer be there to protect the city. The last ocean would boil away and the city would be burned down with it, all life destroyed.

The last life on a dying planet.

With tears welling up in his eyes, Carc turned away and walked to a pressure door leading out of the agricultural dome. He did not bother to close the door. Beyond it, there was a corridor leading to another section of the small city, a geodesic dome built on the ocean floor a hundred metres from the agricultural dome. It was one of the five habitation modules that made up the city and the last one he was to visit. There was one more stop to be made before he headed for the hangar and his ship.

The most important cultural treasure in the city was its historical museum. At least it was so to Carc. The building had once held treasures and relics telling the story of the entire history of the planet, from the ancient era when people had still lived on the continents under direct sunlight – as absurd as the idea sounded to modern ears – to the eons that the underwater habitats had been the only place where life could still exist.

Carc had worked at the museum when it had still been open. He had designed and set up exhibitions of holographic visualisations of daily life as it had once been, of relics that had been preserved for eons, of animals and peoples that had inhabited the planet during its garden era. And the vast submerged habitat construction projects that had been undertaken when the sun had grown hotter as it ran lower and lower on hydrogen.

The museum had never been very popular. The people living under the oceans were not keen on being reminded of the time when their ancestors had lived under the open skies. They did not want to see images of plants and flowers that no longer existed, learn of animals that had been hunted down for food in the last frenzy for survival, or hear descriptions of the fresh air and wind that people had once been able to enjoy.

The exhibitions had been shut down and the great rooms stood empty, only dust and litter remained on their floors. The physical relics were all gone and the most valuable holoprojectors had been removed. Some of them might be unpacked and used again aboard one of the vast generation ships that had been built to allow the population to flee the doomed star system. That is, Carc thought in anger, if anyone cared enough to reserve room for such an unimportant cause as the entire history of the planet that had birthed the fleeing species.

Would they prefer just to forget their past, as they had when they moved to live on the bottoms of the oceans?

It was to battle such ignorance that he had made his own arrangements. He could not trust anyone else to care enough for their cultural heritage to want to preserve it. Even though the Council had made a point of packing away the museum artifacts, they did not care for them the way Carc did. They had not breathed life into those relics every day for their entire lives. Many of them had never even visited the museum.

He had checked.

He had made copies of all of the holoshows ever created over the history of the museum and stored them aboard his own spaceship. The work had taken years and, during that time, he had found presentations made by his predecessors that he had never even heard of. Documentaries of aspects of life that he had not known to exist. Treasures, every one of them.

But they were treasures easy to copy, easy to preserve and share with others. Every copy was as valuable as the original. That was not the case with the true relics: the physical artifacts. Sure, you could scan and make copies of them, but even the best reproductions lacked that one thing that made the originals stand out: the knowledge that someone, long ago, had made and used them in a world vastly different from what was known today.

Carc walked to the middle of a small, empty room. The room had held an exhibition of some of the rarest and oldest artifacts, from an era when people had used their hands to create their tools and no machinery had existed. Most of the items now lay in the cargo holds of the generation ships and Carc had shed many a tear thinking that no one would ever open those crates to see what was inside. And, even if they did, they would not understand the true value and importance of the lovingly preserved relics.

He knelt down and opened a section of the floor. The opening had once housed a holoprojector, but now it held a simple long box. He picked it up and laid it on the floor beside him. It was the last of such boxes that he had hidden away from the workers who had emptied the museum, the last of the twelve boxes that he could not trust into the hands of anyone else. The generation ships would only carry copies of the items. It was all that the masses there deserved. The real artifacts would be safe aboard his ship, to be shared only with people whom he had taught to honour his legacy.

His hands shook when he reached for the locks that held the box shut. The box itself was a relic, made of wood that had grown on one of the old continents. It had been carefully preserved by generations upon generations of specialists. His fingers caressed the oiled surface as they slid onto the archaic mechanical locks. They clicked open, releasing the lid.

Carc sat still on the floor, steadying his breath before he lifted the lid and marvelled at the contents of the ancient box.

The object had once been a weapon, used by ancient peoples to threaten and kill each other. But that had been its purpose for only two or three decades at most. Far more important was the function that it had served for the billion years that had followed. A relic of an era long forgotten, of peoples no longer existing: The first intelligent species on the planet when it had still been young. Species that had hardly understood the notion that the sun that made their lives possible would some day kill their world.

Carc reached for the object and touched it with his bare hand for the first time in his life. The steel was cool, smooth and oily. He moved his hand to the handle and lifted the item, feeling the weight of its history.

The people who had made it had been the first to call themselves humans. They had lived in an era when the planet had been at its best: a beautiful garden world full of species of animals and plants that he could hardly imagine. They had been a violent species and had made many tools of death and destruction. They had even tried to destroy the very world upon which they lived, but had only achieved their own demise. Other species had followed them, learning from the relics that the humans had left behind and lifted themselves towards intelligence. Some had been violent and others benevolent. Some had been long-lived, while others had died off before they had reached their full potential.

But despite the fact that they were all gone now, they had all been part of the wonder that had been planet Earth.

Carc put the sword back into its box and closed it. Then, carrying the box, he walked through the museum corridors for the last time. His fur prickled in sadness as he listened to the echoes of his steps in the empty rooms.

The last guardian of Earth's past.

MARKO is a Finnish teacher educator and a writer, published in anthologies and magazines. He's got a PhD in education sciences and likes to dress up as a 17th century swordsman.

Follow his blog here: http://susimetsa.blogspot.com/

Eternal

by Shaun Gibson

The long goodbye was hard. It began with Angela. When she died in her eighty-third year, my last ties were gone. My sons, now getting older themselves had grown children of their own. I began the main project of programming the telescope and then said my farewells to my children and grandchildren. They don't understand why I want to go. Sometimes, you just need to know and as my life nears its end, I'll have the privilege of learning the answers, even if I can't share them.

I've lived a long and full life and I'm proud of it, here at the end. I've made mistakes, I've been selfish at times, but on the whole it's been a good life. I've contributed to the well-being and happiness of those around me: my family, my wife, my two sons and their children. And I've had a successful career, so successful that I'm able to fund this one last quixotic research project. I have enough curiosity left in me to want to know the truth. But sadly I'll be the only one to know what I find. Rules are made to be broken, they say. But there's a rule of nature that is the exception. What goes into a black hole doesn't come out.

The Last Truth drops out of hyperspace and I get my first look at the system unofficially designated 'Little Beast'. I've obviously seen images of it in my research, but to see it with my own eyes is another experience entirely. Officially designated V4641 Sagittarii the system contains two celestial bodies and millions of miles of hot stellar atmosphere arcing through space spiraling in from the normal star to its neighbor, the black hole that gives the system its unofficial name.

Once massive, it originally condensed into a neutron star, but the pull on two of its neighbors kept it supplied with material and a few million years ago, a crisis pushed the neutron star over the edge. One of the neighbors finally surrendered to the continuous gravitational pull and was hauled in. And the Little Beast was born. The same fate, being eaten in return for years of feeding, awaits its surviving neighbor, but not for millions of years. The arcing jets of hot stellar gas swirl around a tiny spherical space. From the poles of this tiny sphere emerge two long spikes, one of which once pointed towards Earth, detected as x-rays, so powerful that they were discovered even in the dark ages before interstellar travel had begun.

The sphere itself is an illusion of course, a well understood phenomenon in nature. The event horizon, a not quite arbitrary cut off point between what the rules of physics say we can see and what we can't. However to a point we can make predictions and model that space using mathematics of the singularity that lies within.

It's ironic that I'm not even the slightest bit interested in what happens inside an event horizon or what lies beyond it. Despite being a physicist the mysteries of singularities and wormholes and parallel universes mean nothing to me. I know the physics and it's nothing more than a group of interesting facts and speculation with no practical applications. I've never been one for bravery or exploration. Humanity has explored enough of the Great Frontier to be satisfied and for the most part, so am I. The physics of black holes, singularities and worm holes makes it clear that these monsters of nature are interesting but there's no way that anyone could make a return trip. Probes have been sent, well-programmed automated ships have gone through and the occasional explorer with the Right Stuff has ventured. However, none has returned and I don't expect to either.

The Last Truth herself is a miracle of modern engineering, nothing like it could have existed even a generation ago. The ship itself is a state of the art yacht, fast, sleek and comfortable, a rich man's plaything. But she isn't what she is for that. Something like her could have been approximated a hundred or even a thousand years ago. It's her shields that make her special, part of that Darwinian back and forth between militaries, based on that now famous quantum gravitational principle of inversion. When they're on, there's very little that can get through them. And militaries aren't happy about that. There are a few specialized weapons that can, but there's nothing in nature. I could take the Truth into the centre of our sun and she'd be fine. The same shielding was used on the probes and ships that were sent through on their exploration missions.

Now if you fall into an average black hole, nothing really special happens. You fall towards the singularity in the middle and if you're equipped you can see the universe outside, but only the light from just after you entered, so it's hardly worth the trip. But I didn't choose the Little Beast because it's one of the closest black holes to Earth. I chose it because it spins.

I've always been interested in beginnings and endings, history, science, mythologies. We know what we can about the beginning of the universe, but even now questions remain about its final fate. And I want to know how this story ends. Angela's final journey allowed me to make my own.

I enter the navigational course into the Truth and she surges forward, fast for now to shorten my trip, I pull in just above the accretion disc and we soar through the light minutes, seconds and hours towards the event horizon. I patch in my telemetry to the solitary research outpost, what they privately think I don't know, but they'll be glad to receive my data. I key in the special telescope and put it on the screen in front of me, programmed to adjust the blue shift.

The people on the research outpost will never see me hit the event horizon. I just start going slower and slower.

I'm beyond the point where they'll care and my transmission will be so red-shifted by now that it's unreadable. I'm really on my own. My engines are now firing at full power to slow my descent as much as possible because I came here for the show.

The research post has gone. I assume there were pilgrimages from sons and grandchildren in their old age. My personal fancy but I don't think I'm wrong. Hundreds of years pass, then thousands, then more.

The Little Beast's companion star shrinks and shrinks and finally gives in to the gravitational pull of my host. Millions of years have passed. The stars around me are no longer the stable points of light they had been during my journey. They pulse, they glow, they spark and sometimes they explode. The sky becomes a living breathing thing. Billions of years pass. The stars of the Milky Way almost seem to dim as something magnificent grows slowly and begins to dominate the sky. Andromeda, its billions-of-years journey towards the Milky Way reaches its climax and the two dance. Chaos reigns as slowly they come together and I'm now far into the future in the Milkomeda galaxy. Things accelerate.

Stars pulse and glow, are born and die or fade away. The whole sky is a pulsing rhythm. I see the other galaxies approach and I know the universe has survived at least one of its predicted great crises. I know things now others of my time can't know. The galaxies dance and the beauty moves me in a way I never expected, as one after another of the forty-seven local galaxies are swallowed into the giant that is Milkomeda. Trillions of years and I know that the black dwarf remnant of my sun has gone, swallowing with it the graveyard of my people. The dance continues and slows and one by one the stars begin to go out.

My own journey nears its end as the Truth finally nears the spinning white singularity at the centre, but I don't care about that. I gaze at those last flickering remnants of the universe as blackness governs and I'm at peace as the Last Truth drifts through the shimmering doorway. What I find there is what I take with me. All things end, even her and I've brought the memory of her here. Nothing lasts forever, but our love is here at the end of all things; of the stars, the galaxies and even the universe itself.

SHAUN GIBSON was born in Dalmellington, Scotland but has lived in Italy since 2002 where he teaches English. Crazy husband of long-suffering wife Mariangela and crazier father to son James.

Fastbreeder

by Pierre le Giue

'None of us knows what's in these here atoms they're dropping down on us.'

Bill the Supreme Dairies foreman was reading his tabloid as we sat at the cheese warehouse door that Lancashire morning in 1961 drinking our brew. Woodplumpton, the works cat named after the village of his birth, stretched sleepily on the step in late October sunlight.

'That Khrushchev with his bomb,' Bill went on.

According to the paper, strontium 90 fallout from the Soviet leader's latest 50 megaton toy had rendered milk undrinkable throughout the northern hemisphere and we faced several days without our essential raw material.

'Daft, isn't it?' he said. 'Gallons of the stuff down the drain twice a day.'

He tipped his white regulation trilby back on his head and carried on reading. I looked up from my *Science Fiction Film Review*.

'If they can't use it, why are they still milking, then?'

Bill put on his 'patient' expression. 'Well, lad, with all their modern science, nobody's yet invented a way of corking cows up.' He added, 'You've still got your shelves to do in there, though.'

I replaced the top on my Thermos, folded the magazine and walked toward the cold store at the back of the main warehouse.

Thick insulated doors swished shut behind me as I entered the dim, cavernous room. I felt the temperature drop. Soon I was up on my stepladder brushing the wooden shelf surfaces between the tubby waxed 50-pound cheeses. Supreme Dairies did not pay high wages, but it was their policy not to lay anyone off, assigning people to cleaning or maintenance tasks when necessary. The milk wagons no longer came to the loading dock, but existing cheese stocks were unaffected and the business of our warehouse went on.

The room lightened as Bill opened the door.

'Make sure you brush up every speck of that cheesemite, lad.'

I looked down at him. His customary pencil sat behind his ear, but he hadn't been whistling one of his old Flanagan and Allen tunes as he came in. He seemed on edge, which wasn't like Bill.

'Sir!' I said with a mock salute to ease the tension, and carried on.

Fluorescent tubes set into the insulated ceiling a foot above my head gave a dim yellow light and I could see across rows of eight-foot-high shelves, shadowy and monolithic. A cold breeze from one of the wall-mounted Kelvinator refrigeration fans ruffled my hair. Three more units, high up near the ceiling, kept up a steady stream of icy air from the room's other corners with a deep drone like a distant zeppelin, soporific despite the cold. It wasn't the kind of serious cold store where people needed fur-lined parkas, though each Kelvinator sported a dribble of ice on the steel mesh covering of its fan blades. Bright October sun glinted through cracks in the door as I brushed the shelves clear of cheesemite amid the background drone.

What we called cheesemite, or just mite, looked like grey dust but it multiplied quickly; a fairly benign infestation. Some people claimed that mites were essential to the maturing process, but however far this was true my job was to brush up any I found, even though a wax coating protected our cheeses. I paused for a moment. Bill had once told me that I'd get a fright if I saw one of them through a microscope.

Looking at the sweepings from my weekly task, there certainly was more of the itchy dust than usual and I was suddenly conscious of all the unseen turmoil going on in that innocuous looking sprinkling.

'*Tishhhhh ... tushhhh ...*'

I stopped as I heard a faint sound. It was close by. Like something pulling in a breath.

Too much science fiction, I thought. My magazine contained a review of a film about an invisible monster detectable only through giant footprints and the sound of deep, heavy breathing. It was nothing. I went back to my work.

'*Tishhhhhh ...*'

This was louder. It seemed to come from all around. The sound was repeated, becoming stronger as if the room itself were breathing. I imagined millions of cheesemites banding together to overwhelm me. Jumping from the ladder, I hurried to the central aisle, nearly tripping over a neat stack of Danish Blue and sundry delicacies. The doors were outlined by narrow chinks of light, I raced towards them counting my steps. Five ... four ... three ... two ... Made it.

Bill looked up as I crashed through into the brightness of the outer warehouse. Beyond the wide sliding door were fields and cows under a blue autumn sky. No sound escaped from the room I had just left. Woodplumpton purred and rubbed his fur against my ankle, sauntering past the door without a second glance. He would have sensed anything dodgy and growled. I suddenly felt foolish and turned to go back in.

'Everything all right, lad?' called Bill.

'Er ... yes thanks, Bill.' I pushed open the thick doors. At once an unbroken metallic chattering filled both rooms.

'Don't worry about that, lad,' said Bill. 'It's just the pipes. Happens every now and then. Have you got all that mite?'

'Nearly,' I said, stepping into the cool room to the sound of refrigeration fluid surging through tiers of copper pipes that lined the walls to supplement the Kelvinators. I picked up my brush and was just starting up the ladder when a shadow crept along the dim floor to my right. Woodplumpton? Too cold for him in here. Another shadow oozed from the left to meet the first. Then, with shelves suddenly boiling with animated grey dust I was off the ladder and bounding for safety through an ankle deep tide of cheesemite.

I burst through the doors to the metallic screech of the works' klaxon, and not the guttural 'wherk wherk wherk' signalling tea breaks and end of shift but one long continuous rasp. I saw Bill staring at something behind me. His finger was hard on the alarm button; a phone in his other hand.

'Out, lad.'

As he shouted, Bill slammed down the receiver and bounded to the cool room door, shooting the bolt just as the insulated panels bulged under the pressure of the force from inside. I sprinted out, Bill on my heels, just before the hinges gave, and Woodplumpton erupted yowling from the building ahead of a churning grey mass that burst through the aperture where the doors had been.

I stared round at Bill for guidance and felt some reassurance that he looked exasperated rather than scared by the turn of events. He managed not only to roll the main door closed but to secure the padlock. Something thudded against the heavy tongue-and-groove planking and the slider track rattled.

Workers were pouring out of the dairy on to the path that led down the side of the building. An unmarked Land Rover with a blue flashing light on its roof turned into the gate and four people in white coveralls and rubber masks jumped out carrying what looked incongruously like domestic vacuum cleaners connected with hoses to tanks on their backs.

Their leader flipped her faceplate up, switched off the quacking radio at her belt and addressed us tersely.

'Everyone into the field. Now.'

Nobody argued, and I looked back to see the warehouse door split, releasing a now familiar grey mass that settled on the ground only to slow and stop after three yards or so. Within seconds the rampant cheesemite had taken on a dead, ash-like appearance. I seemed to be the only one who noticed the small grey mass that stirred before splitting from the main volume and sliding away under the hedge. I told Bill what I had seen.

'They'll not get far on their own, lad,' he said. 'We had all this in 1957 with those other pesky atoms from Windscale.'

A word with the Land Rover team and two suited figures jogged off across the field carrying their vacuum-like appliances and a transparent plastic bin, only to return in an agitated state.

'That big dose has done it this time,' one called. 'Some of them are getting too clever.'

The leader spoke into her walkie talkie and five minutes later a military looking helicopter flew over, disappearing in the direction of the breakaway mass. We dispersed, and next morning the only sign of the previous day's excitement was a joiner repairing the doors. Woodplumpton was back at his post in the doorway, and there was no cheesemite on the shelves. With milk deliveries and cheese production renewed, life soon returned to normal.

'Well, lad,' said Bill. 'Seems to me they're going to have to keep a better eye on their atoms after this,' and there the matter ended.

Except that I still experience a *frisson* of unease whenever an occasional faint *'Tishhhh'* whispers through the cool room pipes.

PETER FORD (writing as Pierre le Gue) is a retired teacher who has been reading, watching and listening to science fiction since childhood. His work has appeared in anthologies, specialist journals and the local press. This is his first of three stories in this collection.

Hope

by David Styles

Hannah held her head in her hands and cried. The future of humanity had rested on her shoulders; it now lay in ruins at her feet.

It had been many years since people had sneered at the suggestion that human activities were having a detrimental effect on their planet. For a while the projected environmental collapse remained a subject of ridicule. In retrospect that time was short, but crucial. By the time it became clear that this wasn't a laughing matter, the damage was done.

The history books told how prediction came true. '*Global Warming*' and '*Sea Levels Rising*' and '*Ozone Depletion*'; originally phrases used by crackpots trying to scare the gullible, evolved into scientific terminology to describe possibilities in computer generated climate models. They became reality; then swear words used by what remained of a helpless human race.

That was the phrase – Hannah remembered her parents already mourning the '*helpless human race*'. Cast adrift on a dying world; ruined by generations long dead. Humanity had found a scapegoat for their misfortunes, given up, and was waiting to die. When hope came it was nearly too late …

Back when the future looked bright, astronomers had found planets of other stars. Scientific techniques, refined over centuries to a very precise art, revealed an amazing amount of information about the thousands of Earth-sized worlds that had been discovered. Many of these were not just Earth-sized. Many would seem to be Earth-like. From the ample data available there were twenty-eight of these worlds within one hundred light years of Earth which were Earth-like enough to be seriously considered as colonisation targets.

Or to be considered as seriously as one could when one knew just how impractical was the entire concept of inter-stellar colonisation.

Hannah's teachers had explained the hopelessness of inter-stellar travel by analogy: a game of basketball. Try throwing a basketball into the hoop. Hannah had tried. It was tricky, but with a little practice she had succeeded, and could do it three times out of four. From a distance of five yards. Her teacher had suggested she tried from the far end of the gymnasium. Before Hannah could protest, the teacher added that a better analogy would be to have the hoop on the moon.

'*Space is big*,' he told her.

He was right. But he was also wrong.

The graduate student who first had the idea was no longer young. Hannah had met him just before the ship had launched. He was in late middle-age now; professor-emeritus of ... what university was he at? A man who'd seen the blue-sky idea of his youth transform the entire world.

How did he describe it? Imagine two points on opposite sides of a sheet of paper. To get from one to the other you could go the long way across and round the sheet of paper, or you could go through the paper. On saying that, he'd thrown up his hands because '*wormholes are impractical*' apparently. Instead of going through the paper, he'd suggested folding it. Or crinkling it, twisting it and replacing the paper with an elastic sheet that would stretch and squash. Then some strange symbols and equations had been scribbled and Hannah had smiled politely.

She'd not really understood the concept when her lecturers at grad school had first expounded it, and few people had ever entirely understood it. But Hannah didn't need to know the details. It was enough that space could be stretched.

Hannah had learned that it was possible to get the basketball into that hoop on the moon; and she wasn't alone in realising this. Humanity seemed to recover, a little, from the torpor that had gripped it for the last century. The old books in the universities were dusted off. Knowledge, not actually lost but no longer understood, was regained by a generation which now studied so hard to be part of the future that they now had.

Whilst many studied, others, equally driven, built.

Only the best of them had been chosen to crew the five star-ships. Star-ships – a clichéd term, but what other name could have been used?

The first had collapsed on launch; collapsed in the same way that a house of cards collapses. How had they explained it? Something to do with the way that HSS-01 'Columbus', being far larger than the test drones, hadn't generated enough energy to compress space adequately.

Hannah had nodded sagely at the explanation given, whilst bravely hiding the tears for the friends with whom she'd trained for so many years. She still didn't completely understand what the experts had told her; talk of wave front tensors left her cold. But she realised that 'Columbus', being the first since the test drones, was an experiment. And even in failing, 'Columbus' had taught its designers so much.

Minor adjustments were made to the four remaining ships. Or so a watching humanity was told; those making the adjustments knew the difference between minor adjustments and major overhauls.

Hannah had watched expectantly as HSS-02 'Da Gama' had presumably launched successfully. One moment the ship was hanging in space, a little further from Earth than the moon, and then it was not. The telemetry was almost exactly as the experts had predicted it would be; there was no reason to suspect anything had gone wrong.

But 'De Gama' was not expected back for some time. The phrase 'some *time* was deliberately vague. Given a successful extra-solar jump *'for want of a better term'*, there was some uncertainty as to exactly where in the Gliese 581 system the ship would arrive. Getting from that point to their target could take years. A cursory survey of what they found would take months.

Those who were of a betting nature expected to see *'Da Gama'* return in about six years; but no one would be surprised if she was gone for ten. Too long to wait before sending out the remaining three ships.

A month later Hannah had again held her breath as HSS-03 *'Battuta'* had set off; if setting off was the correct term for something which just vanished. Where was *'Battuta'* going? The letters and numbers they'd used instead of a name for a star meant nothing to her.

But *'Battuta'* had set off according to plan.

Six weeks later Hannah felt physically sick. Watching one ship collapse and two launch successfully had been nerve-wracking. But now it was her turn, she and the other five brave souls who crewed HSS-04 *'Zheng He'*.

Launching was an anticlimax. One moment they were in space with Earth and moon hanging in the near distance. There was a sensation akin to tripping over a step, and Earth and moon were gone.

They soon identified the star 47 Ursa Majoris which was to be their Sun for the next few years, and within two hours they located the Jupiter-like world to which they immediately made their way.

That planet was no good to humankind; but the Earth-sized moon in orbit around it certainly was. Or so it had seemed from many light years away. HSS-04 *'Zheng He'* had been sent to make sure. Hannah had a wry smile at the realisation that they could travel ten light years in an instant, but would now take a year to travel a few astronomical units to their final destination.

'Zheng He' had been equipped with two landing craft; capable of touching down on any terrestrial surface, be it ice, rock, sand, land or

water. One was sent down with half of the crew – three of them – to make a preliminary survey. It had landed; or more precisely '*watered*' on an ocean and had sailed to the nearest beach where the crew had immediately reported a breathable atmosphere; if smelling somewhat odd. Video footage showed lush vegetation, and odd looking things of various sizes that were probably animals. Hannah watched with excitement as the ground crew left their lander to investigate the shore line.

She never saw what happened. The shore party scrambled over some rocks; they went behind a rather large boulder which obscured the camera's view, and never emerged. With trembling hands Hannah deployed a remotely controlled blimp. Its camera showed the bloodied bodies of her friends lying behind that large rock.

The remaining crew turned to her. Should they go down or not? What alternative had they? To go home and report failure? She ordered her fellow two crewmates into the remaining lander. But those meteorologists weren't pilots so Hannah remotely piloted the vessel, as she had in countless simulations.

The sight of the small craft inexplicably impacting into the calm ocean had etched itself into Hannah's memory.

Had her crewmates tried to take over control of the lander when the turbulence started?

Was it equipment failure?

Was it her incompetence? Hannah held her head in her hands and cried. The future of humanity had rested on her shoulders; it now lay in ruins at her feet.

DAVE STYLES – husband, father and grandfather. Biomedical scientist by trade, has been bitten by anacondas and tigers, and was voted "Kent Geocacher of the Year 2015". This is the second story by David in this collection.

Follow his life at: http://mankybadger.blogspot.co.uk/

Hybrid Dreams

by Stuart Aken

Every morning of Luce Quain's life, the sun had risen in spectacular fashion from the night's receding rain clouds. The only variation was the time of rising and its location relative to her current place of residence.

'See that? Do anything for you?' He pointed through the window, clearing its nightly opacity to allow the daylight in.

She glanced up from beside him. 'Used to, in the early years. But after four hundred odd years, even the spectacle of a colourful sunrise can become banal.'

'I wondered. You never said. Four hundred. That'll be why you're such an expert. How many have you had?'

She studied him, looked into those eyes that had first drawn her to this strange man. 'Not seeking a comparison, then? Unusual. Most men want to know. But when I saw you in this idiosyncratic home, I knew you'd be different in other ways.'

He made no reply, but studied her with the air of the artist she'd found him to be. She watched the thoughts skim across his face, saw the assessment, the challenge he faced.

'If you like.'

He smiled, then. Nodded.

'How, and when?'

His gesture told her to rise, sit on the edge of the bed, and she did. His hands folded her in the air and she copied their movement until he stopped and she felt she was echoing his wants. 'That's how, Luce. When? After breakfast?'

They ate at his table. Hand made. From wood he'd collected in the stand of trees over by the stream he used for bathing. Afterwards, drinking the steaming liquid he called tea, served in his crafted mugs, she watched him grind pigment and mix it with oil extracted from one of the plants in his garden.

'Does that have to stand guard?'

Luce looked at her droid, impassive in the corner, awaiting her commands. 'Not now I know you.' She turned to the android, 'Go outside and recharge in the sunshine, Monster.'

To the untutored eye, the machine was as human as its owner. It nodded at her and walked into the garden, stood in the sunshine and removed its minimal covering to gain maximum exposure to the sunlight.

'He's harmless, you know. Unless I indicate he should be otherwise.'

'Whatever it was that happened to you, to make you use that … that abomination, it's still there in your eyes, Luce. And that thing's an "it" not a "he".'

'Not to me.' She neglected to let him know she'd designed the prototype and modified this particular one to her own specifications. Monster was now her servant in all ways a woman could want.

'Doesn't it embarrass you with its servile manner?'

She ignored the jibe. 'You're a throwback, you know.'

'Maybe. You don't think I might be the future instead, Luce?'

She did. But, in the game of gender politics she'd been programmed to employ since puberty, it didn't do to submit too easily to the object of desire. So, she didn't let him know. After all, once genetic manipulation had reduced the hunt to mere formality, how was a male to impress the female he intended to seduce, if not with his prospects?

'It's still there, Luce. You're right. The male need to breed still functions. The genetic imperative to spread our genes goes on even through the modifications of your scientists.'

'My scientists? I am a scientist.'

He nodded. 'Beauty and brains.'

'You assumed I was a standard Sexual.'

'I never assume. And to call you "standard" goes against the evidence of my eyes, and our experience.' He took her hand and walked her toward the place he'd have her pose.

'I'm a hybrid: Intellectual with Sexual. It's what my parents chose for me. Father wanted me to have fun; Mother wanted me to have respect.'

'A hybrid dream, then. I bow to your parents' choices.'

'You're a Creative, of course.' Her confidence made him smile.

'I'm a Natural.'

She stopped in her tracks, a feat she'd read of but never experienced. It was a momentary interruption to their saunter, but one destined to develop into revelation.

'Not repulsed, then?'

How could she be? He'd passed through that tunnel many years before. In any case, she'd been as intimate with him as a woman could be with a man. And he'd been unusually deft, unusually attentive, unusually caring. A pleasantly singular experience amongst a long, long list of otherwise similar encounters. 'Intrigued.'

He nodded and persuaded her to sit on the small outcrop, wild water flowing to her left, the stand of trees behind her. She took up the pose he'd mimed in the room he kept his bed. Not a bedroom really, but a place for rest and sex.

He set up a wooden tripod stand he called an easel, took a flat of coarse material stretched on a wooden frame and placed it on the stand. Also, from his bag, made of the same rough stuff, he took his paints in pots, his handmade brushes and his flat oval of glazed white earthenware.

She watched him paint her. In all her centuries, no one had ever painted her. Imaged, through their various devices, of course. Recorded her in motion both alone and with whatever man she shared her pleasures. But to place her on the surface he called canvas and depict her in colours and strokes she'd seen in virtual displays of art; that was new.

'My scientists.' She savoured the phrase. 'You reject the world around you, then?'

He frowned and stuck the brush between his teeth only to allow him freedom to sweep the scene about them with his unencumbered hands. She watched him return to painting.

'I see. This is your world. But you accept the way we control the weather, and the climate. And you're happy to take advantage of the science that perfected me.'

He paused a moment. Studied her; a scrutiny that would have had a less than perfect specimen squirming with doubt. 'Your mix of genes gives you beauty and a style of sexual attraction I've not come across before.' He smiled at the ancient pun and she did too. 'It's given you long life as well, maybe even eternity: I gather your cells can recover from almost any type of damage?'

'I am, to all intents and purposes, eternal, yes.'

He nodded and continued painting her. 'As for the weather; I'm in the world and can't escape the environment your science dumps on me. If I could choose, I'd have storms and snow and wind and ice. But I have to live with what you and your cronies have caused. Peerless blue skies during the day, rainclouds pouring rain overnight, growing the vegetation and filling reservoirs and streams. It's boring, but it makes what the average man … person, might call paradise. Changeless habitat's not natural. Life can even be defined by the changes that happen to it.'

'You disapprove. You were eager enough to share the pleasures science has provided in my body. Eager enough to paint me now.'

He shook his head. 'When the choice is reduced, the only option is to make the best of it.'

'Reduced choice? There are lots of us; women like me, and men. We're all different and ...'

'You're all the same. You may look different; all showing the careful design of those who think science can do better than eons of evolution. Oh, you and your sort are beautiful, I'll give you that, Luce. Beautiful, desirable, perfect even. But maybe, as human beings, we actually prefer the little faults nature builds into us. Maybe we enjoy those signs of individuality; moles and freckles, uneven features, hair that goes wild, bits that are just too big, or too small.'

'You'd swap perfection of design for natural selection and its random faults?'

He nodded just once. 'Doesn't mean I don't find you beautiful and wantable. Just that I prefer works of nature to those of conservative scientists. Nature's been designing us for millennia. Your scientists have been doing the job only a few hundred years. It's arrogant to claim such recent progress is better than the slower, environmentally-based, work of nature.' He held up a hand, paintbrush pointing between two fingers. 'Yeah, I know nature makes mistakes, forms imperfect patterns, even distorts and deforms from time to time. That happens in experiments. I wonder how many unknown foetuses failed to come to term in your scientists' flasks and tubes.'

'You think we're unimaginative. Conservative. That's how you described scientists.'

'I think searching for physical perfection has driven your creators into a dead end. They make types that match a pre-ordained norm within narrowly defined bounds. You, though, with your intellect to boost the confidence caused by your beauty, you, Luce, manage to be different.'

'I'm not that different from my peers.'

'You've discarded your crystal, glass and graphene Malls for the uncertainties of the natural world, Luce. That labels you a rebel.'

She moved and saw his frown at her change of pose. 'I'm bored. Can we pause?'

He smiled and held out his hands in resignation. She stood and dived straight into the river, swimming a good way beneath the clear surface and rising again midstream. She beckoned and he abandoned his easel to join her.

The water refreshed them both and they left it to allow the sunshine to dry them as they lay together in the lush green grass.

'Come on, wanton, we've work to do if I'm to finish your portrait.' He rose and stretched down to help her to her feet.

'Fuck me first.'

'Insatiable. Not till I've put a few more strokes on to canvas. Up. Sit. Be patient.'

'Ooh, so masterful. Anyone would think your natural existence here alone had made you revert to your ancestral caveman type.'

'On the rock, wench. Sit and stay still. When I've finished the outline …'

But she was already moving off. 'Have to catch me if you want me to sit still.'

He moved toward her. She moved further back.

'Behave yourself, or I'll …'

Her expression said it all. No threat from him was to be taken seriously but she was going to have her fun. She turned and ran, knowing he would chase. There was an innocent thrill in running from a man she trusted, knowing that his eventual capture of her would result in what she wanted.

They ran across the open field and he chased her toward the house: the bed was so much more comfortable than the hard ground, after all.

In the garden, she saw Monster, still taking in the sun, though his recharging session must have finished hours ago. She ran to hide behind the powerful figure, adding an extra element of primeval protection to her fantasy of danger in the wild.

The artist was just steps behind her, desire now guiding him and promising surrender would produce the very thing she wanted. 'Don't think that lump of electronic trash will save you from your fate. I'm going to drag you to my room and have you any way I wish, wench.'

'Ooh, Monster, save me from the rampant man.'

It happened so fast she couldn't take it in at first. He lay at Monster's feet, dark red fluid pooling from the wound the rock had made. She knelt. Took a lifeless wrist to feel a pulse that never came. Monster froze into a state of shock and suddenly she knew she'd lose him too, if she didn't intervene. His built-in prime directive never to kill would force him into self-destruct. She couldn't have that happen.

'It was an accident, Monster. A miscalculation. The flowers hid the rock, you couldn't know there was that danger. You didn't kill him. You were merely doing what you were designed to do: saving me from danger. It was not your fault.'

She watched the changes in his face. The android reasoned and agreed with her analysis. He stopped the process that would end his sentience. It never occurred to Luce that, free of proper human emotion, he should have come to her conclusion more swiftly than she had herself.

Together, she and her trusted guardian gathered up the evidence. The easel and the paints and the half-completed portrait that showed her as he had seen her, and his bag of artist's materials from the river bank.

'CenCon will already know he's ceased to live, Luce.'

'Yes. The implant. I know, Monster. We have to make it look like a different sort of accident. I can't be associated with a death like this. I'm already wanted anyway. Take him into the house. I'll bring the other things.'

She dressed again and Monster walked beside her as they left the scene that might have been a place she could find happiness for a while. The flames and smoke would make conclusion simple, should the sparse authorities find manpower or time to investigate. In practice, it was likely to be recorded as a domestic accident, the artist made one more statistic.

Only when they were well away and on a different island of the English Isles, did she allow her emotions the free rein she'd denied them at the scene. There, survival and pragmatism had taken over; a product of her genetic modelling. But now, out of danger, another aspect of her being was allowed precedence and the emotional element included in her father's package of genes, came to the fore. Monster cradled her as she wept away her sorrow and distress. So much promise lost so easily and quickly.

It would be weeks before the loss softened and took its rightful place amongst her vast compendium of memories. But life would go on. Pleasure would return. And so would fear, of course.

'Will I ever find what I'm looking for, Monster?'

'Only when you know what it is you seek, Luce.'

His insight startled her. Was her guardian developing and growing? But he was right. To find what she was looking for she must first know what it was. And, with a clarity that made the recognition into revelation, she knew.

'I want a man to be with for the rest of time, Monster. And I want a child, a proper child, born of my body, not manufactured in a lab from seed and egg, but made in love and nurtured in my womb. Is that so very strange?'

Monster considered her question. 'Unusual in these hedonist days of your race, Luce. But an inevitable response to the recent death. Your witnessing of such an end has brought your natural human desire to reproduce your genes to the surface of your mind. And your biological imperative, now roused, will lead you to fulfil that natural purpose, more or less regardless of personal cost.'

She looked at the magnificent specimen of manhood caste in plastic, graphene and a multitude of other artificial materials, and nodded at the logic he expressed. The question now, though, was how she'd find the ideal man to share her life and plant the seed she now needed to grow.

'Come, Monster. There's a world out there and, somewhere, there's a man who'll be the right one for my dreams.'

They set out, side by side, toward the far horizon.

One of our professional contributors, STUART AKEN writes at the keyboard as if possessed, which he probably is!

Website: stuartaken.net

Twitter: @stuartaken

If We Start Killing

by Ulla Susimetsä

'If we don't do it, we die.'

'Perhaps it's meant to be. We've come to the end of our existence.'

'The end!' Vanh Jäärä, the Chair of the Council, growled. 'You know the word, don't you? You understand its implications?'

Lintu didn't back down under the verbal lash, highly unusual and unmannerly though it was in the white serenity of the council chamber.

'Everything we are, our glorious civilizations, creations of great minds – the books we wrote, the thoughts we developed, works of art – all will be forgotten.' Jäärä gestured at the holo-walls and their timeless masterpieces. 'Our species will become extinct.'

'That doesn't justify it!' Lintu leapt to her feet, hands balled into fists, shaking. 'What you want to do is … genocide!'

The Chair sliced air with his hand. 'They're an inferior species, and–'

'That's an old argument. It's never been a *good* one. Taking over their bodies, turning them into our hosts, however less evolved they are, however primitive … it isn't right!'

Jäärä stared at her. His eyes were hard, but there was neither greed nor malice in them. Then his anger drained. His shoulders sagged as if under a burden. She barely heard his words: 'But it is our last hope.'

That was the end of discussion. Every Council member, except Lintu Laulula, supported the motion. She spoke again, reminded the

Council of the consequences, appealed to their conscience. But in the end ... in the end, it was their future that was at stake.

Jäärä was right. They were dying. An unknown illness ate them up from inside. And it spread fast. Every second someone succumbed to it and died. Their advanced medical knowledge, their elaborate technology – useless. There was no cure. Experts in every field worked day and night, desperate to save the species, to discover a solution.

They found one. Or millions, as it was.

Lintu had discovered them, long before the plague struck. Remembering the thrill still made her shiver. That was why she was a scientist: the rush, the exhilaration of discovering something hitherto unknown. But this ... *this* was something that blew your mind.

She had observed this new species from afar – craved to make contact, but it was not yet time. They weren't ready.

They were so like her, these creatures. In their biological, physiological makeup. Procreation, motivation, social structures, even the ways they communicated. The civilizations and cultures they had created, the monuments they built to celebrate their achievements. They worked, they played, they made, they ate. They loved, lost, grieved. An ancient, everlasting fantasy, to discover something like them in the infinite expanse of space ... but had anyone ever truly believed it would happen? Hoped, yes; feared, too.

From those feelings sprang fiction, but the truth ... unimaginably strange.

Lintu had discovered them, this species that became their last hope. Her protectiveness was natural.

A useless sentiment, Jäärä had said. She should feel protective towards her own kind, not these ... aliens.

But the aliens were helpless, vulnerable.

They were also capable of terrible things, of slaughtering one another, wrecking cities and civilizations and nature, wasting valuable resources.

The familiarity was heart-breaking. She'd never yet encountered a species that had not, at some point during their existence, done things too horrible to name.

But did that mean they didn't deserve to live?

Blood stained her own people's history. Dark deeds, unmentionable ... yet not even millennia of silence could erase the past. And so they did what any highly evolved species would: they learned from their mistakes. A learning process of generations brought them here, to harmony with each other and their surroundings. Conflicts were resolved without violence. Environment and nature were treasured. Life's myriad manifestations were acknowledged, admired, respected.

But if we do this ... if we start killing ... A spiral back to days of low morals and cruelty, to the times when the strong could do what they wanted to the weak and no one stood in their way.

Despair drove them to their greatest scientific feat. They developed the technique for what was called *transfer*. The Council members and the chancellor were invited to inspect the facility: the equipment, the protocol, the principles. This was Lintu's chance to stop it. The Council had made its decision, but the chancellor could veto the plan.

The enormous facility was dominated by glassy, levitating control panels. Tiny pocket drones flitted around while white robotic arms hummed, engaged in painstaking work where no errors were allowed.

'We have observed the hosts,' said Arlos Gyroge, the scientist who had invented the method, 'placed witchips into each specimen's brain. They're unaware of it, of course; those whose memories retain traces of the experience tell tales of alien abduction.'

Everyone laughed.

Gyroge smiled. 'Naturally, no one believes them.'

When the time came, all that was needed was a single command, and the minds of their hosts would be destroyed. They called it *wiping*. The term didn't change anything.

'To survive, some species require a host,' Gyroge explained. 'The principle is nothing new. We've found a suitable host species, whose physiological properties resemble our own. Erect posture, dexterous fingers, a large brain, and so on. Assimilation should cause no difficulties.'

'But we will be … parasites.' The chancellor curled her lip. 'How could we degrade ourselves–'

'Better to be a parasite than dead.'

'Exactly. And I want to emphasise that the procedure is perfectly safe. No complications should arise from … inhabiting … the bodies–'

'You mean killing,' Lintu said. 'We murder our hosts.'

'Is that true?' the chancellor snapped.

'No, no, we won't be murdering anyone! They will suffer no physical harm in the process – we need their bodies intact, after all. We will simply … occupy them with new minds. Souls, if you will, although the existence of such an entity has never been proved.'

'Looking at this plan, I don't believe we have souls!'

'Calm down, Council member Laulula,' Jäärä intervened. 'This is neither time nor place for remonstration.'

'Then what is?' She whirled on him. 'You can't seriously contemplate this? How could we live with ourselves?'

'I admire your high morals!' Impossible to say whether Jäärä was mocking her. 'Another proof of how evolved we are.'

'See,' Gyroge said, 'it's us who deserve to live on! By replacing their inferior minds with our own, we'll do a service to these miserable little …'

'A service?' Lintu shrieked. 'You call eliminating–'

'The chancellor,' Jäärä hissed, 'needs Council members' advice. Rational, logical advice! Emotional outbursts–'

'I'm not being emotional! I'm trying to stop you from making a mistake. A mistake that …' She shook her head. Had no words. 'If we do this … we'll regret it forever.'

'Regret saving ourselves? Hardly.'

'We will know that it was wrong. It will cast a shadow over us. We do this to preserve our glorious civilizations? We're nothing but savages, wiping out others while seeking our own good!'

'Anyone in our position,' the chancellor said, 'would do the same thing.'

No! Lintu gasped for breath. Didn't want to believe it.

'The plague spreads. It spares no one.' The chancellor sighed. 'We must save ourselves, and this is the only way.'

The day of transfer. The facility loomed before Lintu. She stumbled, forced her trembling legs to walk on. Her heart fluttered in her throat. *There's a name for this: treason.*

But who would live to judge her?

'Council member Laulula.' She showed her ID and lied, 'The chancellor sent me.'

As if she were outside her body, Lintu watched herself walk through the doors. Would this depersonalization continue, once the program was implemented? Life in a strange body …

The device fitted inside her fist. Easy to trigger; just three short squeezes.

Gyroge came, spoke to her. She saw the scientist's lips move, didn't hear a word. Nodded anyway. Did he see the beads of sweat prickling her forehead?

Once Lintu squeezed the device, it would blow up. It would demolish the facility. The species she'd discovered would be safe.

While her kind … they would die of the plague in a matter of days. They who had thought themselves invincible, indestructible, supreme in strength and intelligence. Who had, in their arrogance, believed that they *mattered* in the universe whose scope, endless, eternal, reduced them to a single dust mote. Eventually, every trace of their existence would vanish.

The device burned Lintu's sweaty hand.

A hand on her shoulder. Guilt shook her, a sharp shock. She whirled around, dropped the device.

'Lintu,' Jäärä said, 'you don't want to do this.'

'No. But I must.'

He shook his head. 'If you were going to, you'd have done it already.'

She stared at the floor, at the harmless-looking deadly device. *Pick it up!* But she didn't move. 'How … how could I do this to them?'

She searched for triumph in Jäärä's eyes. Found instead understanding … and pain. 'You're only human.'

ULLA is a Finnish writer, published in anthologies and magazines. When she's not reading or eating chocolate, she's wielding her Viking sword or wrestling with words — writing or translating.
Blog: Wrestles With Words: http://ususimetsa.blogspot.fi/
Facebook: https://www.facebook.com/ullasusimetsa/
Twitter: @ususimetsa

Indirect Harm?

by John Harper

Wet branches snapped as the Tin-head crashed through the undergrowth, an unnatural glow emanating from its barrel body, sunlight reflecting off its shoulder plates.

The beep from Dekker's necklace faded as the Tin-head disappeared from sight. He waited another second then burst from his duck blind. He slipped down the gully after it, insects buzzing around his head, vision spinning from dehydration. He pulled on sodden roots to guide his descent, refusing to slow.

He paused at the bottom, trying to contain his ragged breath as he listened. Ahead the fronds swung like doors on broken hinges, a clear path of mechanical destruction. To the left, the whir of distant servos, the crush of twigs under hydraulics.

He ran, scrabbling over the muddy roots and stones, knife clenched in his fist, spots splashing his vision like distant fireworks.

Each breath dried his desiccated throat. How long had he been running? His entire life? This was the last of the Tin-heads. Only after could he rest. He could still feel his daughter's charred body in his arms, so small and fragile, burnt to a feather-light husk, still feel the tears that had coursed down his face as he had stumbled through the shattered city.

He gripped the knife harder, re-opening the crusted blisters. He'd buried her below a cross made from hydraulic struts and titanium limbs. *Almost over, honey, almost over.*

The trees cleared to a stony river, water gushing as it foamed over a drop then flowed around the bend. His tongue swelled in his mouth. As he dropped to one knee and scooped up water with his hand, his necklace beeped.

He jerked upward. The Tin-head stomped off the far bank, past leafy ferns and out of sight. Dekker leapt into the water, already picturing his knife slicing the Tin-head's vulnerable power cable. The water was cool, flushing away heat and pain. It rose to his knees, pushing him downstream. A green stone moved under his foot and a thud rumbled below him, slow and distorted by the water.

Adrenaline burst through his chest. He turned, wrenching his momentum away from the snare.

He saw blinding light, his ears rang and he flew upward. The geyser of water burst below then above, then the stony bank raced toward him.

The burble of water compressed into wails of pain from all around him. He blinked back the fog, saw bars before him, and beyond that, darkness.

He couldn't move, crushed inside his cage. Human excrement wrinkled his nose, watered his eyes. Behind him, a scream, loud and mortal, then dying to a whimper.

There was something in the darkness. The chorus of sobs stopped mid breath as it drew closer. He could feel it, right there before him. But there was no heat, no life. Just darkness. Empty, hollow darkness. Somewhere a bird tweeted ...

Stones pressed against Dekker's face and he lurched upward. He spat out pebbles red with his blood and rolled over. He blinked in the shafts of sunlight. A blue bird tweeted then fluttered past to land in a nest of rags and bones. He chastised himself for not suspecting a snare. Indirect harm was the only weapon the Tin-head's programming allowed. His only edge.

Servos whirred from across the river, then the wet snap of young branches. He craned his head forward. The Tin-head pushed through the greenery. Necklace beeping, Dekker wobbled to his feet, scooped up his knife and followed the river's edge. The Tin-head weaved in and out of view, an arm servo there, the glow of his radioactive power pack there, but always sticking to the river. Why?

Dekker ran harder. He vaulted over a log peppered with toadstools, slapped dripping ferns aside, then the river turned and the necklace quietened. The chirps of lizards and the sigh of the wind swallowed the fading mechanical sounds.

He almost tripped over the shoulder of a low bridge. He stopped, unable to believe his luck. He stepped around and on to the arch of mortared stones. He stopped before a depression at the bridge's centre. Square in shape, big enough for two feet, recessed half an inch.

Another snare. An easy one. He raised his foot to step around. He froze.

Too easy.

He looked up.

Strung between two bent Kauri trees hung a rope net filled with boulders. He bent down. The forest canopy swayed under a whistling breeze, light catching a filament stretching across the bridge at knee height.

He realized he was holding his breath. He stepped back, hyperventilating. Then he ran, leaping at the last moment. His toe felt resistance and then he was through. A smash pounded behind him and a giant crack, like God's hammer, echoed through the trees. Water plonked in the one-two punch of heavy impact, debris pelted his back and then he left the bridge behind.

He had a daughter to avenge. And prey to catch.

The stony riverland surrendered to a slimy carpet of liverworts as he scurried up the shallow incline. He weaved past hooked roots, jagged stones and black rotting logs. The trees became sparse, their branches starting higher and higher up the trunks until he imagined himself a flea running between the brown hairs of a dog. His short gasping breaths echoed back at him, sharp staccato blasts like an out of tune machine gun.

The incline steepened, the trees parted and he entered a clearing before a cliff. The robot stood beside a recharge node, a square metal cube seemingly grafted to the dirt, covered in an array of solar mats and conduit. The robot either didn't see Dekker or simply realized running was now hopeless. Dekker stepped forward, warm blood coursing through his arms, his grip on the knife tightening, a dark smile on his blistered face. His necklace bleeped in sync with his steps.

'Thought you'd run home, Tin-head? Thought you'd be safe here?'

Dekker closed on his prey, years of pursuit, sweat and blood leading to this final victory. He almost wanted to crow. *This is for you, Angela.* Here stood the last of the last, its composite head tilted downward, almost penitent. His necklace's chirps bled into a continuous tone. He focused on the cabling between the head and the sturdy chest barrel. One quick swish, his life's purpose over.

'Do you feel fear, Tin-head?' he said, taking another step. He studied the twin chasms of emptiness astride its head, the portals to its soulessness.

'I wish I could teach it to you. To watch your own child boil alive in front of you. To be paralysed with fear. To know that you have failed at your sole purpose in life as her protector!' He ran forward and slashed out with his knife.

The Tin-head's arm shot outward, clamping to Dekker's necklace.

The knife split the power cables. Something screeched inside the Tin-head. Its two eyes dimmed as they stared through him. The red light faded from its chest.

Dekker sagged in the Tin-head's dead grip. It was over.

Then the Tin-head spoke, a tinny voice stretched out of all human shape.

'Warning: Reactor overload imminent. Ten seconds to meltdown.'

Dekker stared. Had he cut the wrong wires?

'Nine.'

His eyes widened. No, it was another snare. The final snare.

'Eight.'

He pulled back but the Tin-head's manipulators were locked to the necklace.

'Seven.'

Both hands on the robot's manipulators, digging, pulling, desperate to break free.

'Six.'

He released the manipulators, stared down at his knife.

'Five.'

He wedged the knife up between his neck and the necklace, breathed deep.

'Four.'

He raked it back and forth, slicing through metal and flesh.

'Three.'

Blood drenched his hand, the knife slipped upward. Pain ricocheted through his chin. He kept slicing.

'Two.'

The necklace snapped. He fell back, scrabbling on hands and feet, backward, backward. He turned to stand.

'One.'

He ran for the far trees.

A fist of wind punched into his back. Thunder roared. He flew.

Burning heat danced across his nerves, his back numb and thick and hard.

The wind dumped him and he rolled toward the cliff, steam rising around him.

He looked back at the crater, a cracked smile forming on his face. A laugh came in a gasp and he turned to face the setting sun. The end of a day, the end of the robots. He staggered to the cliff edge, his mind finally clear, as the sunset warmed his sore body.

Light reflected from below. He shielded his eyes.

Below the cliff, nestled across a river delta were rows upon rows of perfect cubes, all of them grafted to the dirt, all of them covered in solar mats.

Recharge nodes.

A robot city.

His bare neck tingled and the memories returned.

It hadn't been a dream.

He wasn't a hunter.

The war was long lost.

He was the prey.

JOHN is a science fiction writer living in Wellington, New Zealand. He likes spending time with his children and is a religious follower of V8 Supercars and the Black Caps Cricket team. By night John is a freelance writer for computer games. By day he works as a chartered mechanical engineer.

Lisa Lives

by Anthony M. Olver

The day began like any other for Lisa Eddington. Mother yelled at her to get out of bed and get ready for school. This morning was better than most, she had 23 minutes until the bus left.

A ticking sound alerted her to hurry. She rubbed the sleep from her eyes, gave her teddy bear a hug, and jumped out of bed. Well, jumped as well as her uncoordinated 12-year-old legs would allow. They somehow tangled themselves and deposited her ungraciously on to the floor rug. Must have had a growth spurt overnight, she thought as she picked herself up off the floor.

'What's that noise?' Mother yelled from the kitchen. 'If you don't get out of that room right now …' The usual array of threats trailed off. Lisa wondered if it was something to do with going to see that Detective yesterday afternoon. Maybe Mother wasn't telling her something and that's why she was being nicer than usual.

Lisa knew that things were pretty tough. The bills were going unpaid. Mother had told her not to answer the telephone. But then yesterday she'd said to Lisa that Detective Colbert from a special police division could help them out of trouble. Lisa couldn't quite remember what Detective Colbert had said. Actually, she couldn't remember much about yesterday at all.

'I'll be out in a minute, Mum,' Lisa called towards the kitchen. She started to pull on her school uniform, but as she reached to zip up the side of her dress she felt a sudden sharp tingling in her left hand. She began gently to massage it. The sensation subsided and she finished dressing.

Arriving in the kitchen she saw a bowl of cereal and a glass of juice on the table. 'What's the special occasion, Mum?'

'You're late, that's what,' Mother replied, pointing to the breakfast.

Lisa ate as quickly as she could, the ticking sound reminding her to hurry. 'This cereal tastes horrible!' Mother gave her a stern look as Lisa struggled to finish it.

After gulping back the last mouthful Lisa rushed to drag a brush through her hair and give her teeth a cursory scrub. 'Get your shoes on, honey,' urged Mother, pulling her ponytail straight, 'or you'll be late for the bus.'

Lisa grabbed her bag and dived for her shoes. Mother always bought them way too big so that she could grow into them, so they were always worn out before they were anything like the right size. But this morning she found herself struggling to squeeze her feet into them. I've definitely had a growth spurt, Lisa thought as she wrestled with the shoes and eventually managed to force her feet into them.

'Bye Mum', Lisa yelled as she threw her school bag over one shoulder and hurled herself the door. 'I'll see you after you get home from work.'

'Be careful, honey,' Mother called back. Lisa wondered what she meant by that as she ran down the path. Mother had never told her to be careful before. Maybe it was something to do with that stranger danger thing she'd heard about at school. A stranger in a van had grabbed a snobby kid from the posh school up the hill and she'd never been seen again. Probably did it to get a huge ransom so she'd heard. She knew that no-one would take her for a ransom, that was for sure.

As she ran she glanced at her watch, horrified to see the numbers

08:26 glaring back at her in a challenge to reach the bus stop in time. She wouldn't be able to make it. The only way to reach the bus stop by 08:30 was to take the short cut. She sprinted across the road towards the park, clambered over the low wall and slid down to the shady track below.

As she scrambled along the track, she heard the sound of running footsteps in the distance behind her, coming closer. The stranger danger rule! She threw her bag into the bushes, and scurried in after it, ducking out of sight as a man in a drab green tracksuit ran past. Lisa waited for a moment, then grabbed her bag and followed after him trying to make up for the lost time.

The track split in two up ahead. One way continued through the park towards the playground near the green square, the other wound its way under the road and came up the other side just near her bus stop. Lisa slowed down as she neared the tunnel. There would be too much traffic to get across quickly. She glanced at her watch. 08:28. The tunnel it was.

She'd heard people talk about the feeling that you get when you're being watched, like the hairs on your body standing on end, or a tingling sensation or some such thing. She was beginning to feel something like that now. The tunnel wasn't long, but there must have been somewhere for him to hide because Lisa didn't see him until he had one arm around her waist, and the other over her mouth.

Shock and fear exploded inside her. She tried to call out, but his hold over her mouth was too tight. Her left arm began to feel numb again. The ticking noise began to get louder, almost drowning what he was saying as he manhandled her to the ground. She saw the glint of a knife blade just before she lost consciousness.

Jack smiled as his latest prey fell limp in his arms. He couldn't believe his luck. This would be the second girl he'd caught in the tunnel this month. He leaned down to smell the soft skin on her neck and gently released his grip on her mouth. As he did so, the girl suddenly straightened up with more force than a girl her age should. Her arm shot out. He felt her hand tight around his throat as the world tipped and he was on his back, the girl pinning him to the ground. He thought he heard a ticking sound as her head rotated to face him. Her eyelids flickered, and for a moment he thought he saw a red glow before her blue-green eyes locked on his. 'You are under arrest for attempted kidnapping. You will not resist. Please hold still.'

He lay there in shock for a moment before he heard a voice say, 'It's okay, Lisa, you can stand down now, we have him.'

Lisa released her grip and stood to attention awaiting her next instruction. She watched Detective Colbert, in his drab green tracksuit, and Mother formalise the arrest of the would-be kidnapper.

'Hello, Mother,' Lisa said as Detective Eddington came over to her. 'Are you proud of me?'

'You did a great thing today, Lisa, we are very proud you. Come on, we'd better get you cleaned up for school.' Detective Eddington put her hand on Lisa's head and activated the reset routine.

'So, your program has had another success, Detective Colbert,' observed Deputy Commissioner Jones. 'Congratulations.'

'The child android program has had some setbacks, sir, but Lisa has proven to be very reliable,' said Detective Colbert. 'Detective Eddington has fulfilled the role of her mother quite well and we believe that we can continue.'

The Deputy Commissioner nodded. 'I agree it's successful so far, but if Lisa sees a white van like the one that kidnapped her, or if she remembers anything about her murder, there could be unforseen consequences. Have you thought about that?' The Deputy Commissioner paused for a moment before continuing. 'Will her programming be stable enough to prevent the real Lisa's consciousness from coming out during an arrest?'

'I hope so sir,' murmured Detective Colbert, 'For Lisa's sake, I hope so ...'

ANTHONY M. OLVER began writing at a young age before discovering that resistance was futile and embarked on a career as an electrical engineer. His wife and two children are very tolerant of his obsession with 8-bit computers and a 30 year old space sim game called Elite.

Web: elitearchives@icloud.com

Twitter: @elitearchives

Man-akin®

by Nici Lilley

I was watching vids when a hot spike of agony in my belly almost stopped my breath. I panted through my nose – tiny ins-and-outs – and when it eased, I carefully put my left hand on my right wrist. Movement aggravated the torment, but I pressed my fingernail into the indentation on the med-bracelet – once, twice – and blessed relief ran around my body, switching off pain receptors. I pressed again, desperate for prolonged respite from the invaders tearing at my insides. It bleeped at me and the display showed orange – too many hits in too short a time.

The adrenaline of anger gave me strength to yell. 'I can make my own fricking decisions. I don't need some stupid *tech* telling me I've had enough. *I* know when I've had enough. I've always known.'

'Clearly not, my dear, or you wouldn't be here, would you?'

I made a rude gesture at whichever arsehole was currently part of the 24/7 observation team, and slowly sat back. The sofa moulded itself to my over-heavy body, and I snapped my fingers twice to activate the floating display. I swished the options to soothing music and let it lull me into a doze.

I woke up howling. The pulsing agony was so severe I could feel sweat sheening every millimetre of my skin. The bracelet let me administer one shot, then it flashed green.

Finally!

I staggered to the prepared cubicle, pulled off my robe and wrapped my fingers around the metal ring half-embedded in the wall for support. The red beams of a body scan lit the room and I closed my eyes against the glare. Eventually the pain eased off to bearable and I paced, holding my belly. I wanted it to be over, but I was so scared, so—

My stomach spasmed as if white-hot barbs were twisting inside it. I hung on to the ring, panting.

'Bear down now.'

'What do you think I'm doing, you fuckwit!'

I pushed and sobbed and yelled and pushed until an ugly sound shut me up. Something slid out of me with a squidgy metallic plop. Another followed, and another, until five things were wriggling wetly on the soft floor.

I didn't want to look. I squeezed my eyes shut, hoping the watchers would come in and remove their creations, so I would never ever have to see them.

Then something touched my foot, and instinctively I looked down.

A scream stuck in my throat. The obscenity was twenty centimetres long from its hairless cranium to its crooked toes. Its polymetal bones glistened beneath translucent silvery skin.

The eyes watching me were the same bright blue as mine.

I wanted to squash it. To trample each travesty to pieces. I even lifted my foot but pain ripped through me again.

The final one emerged.

It landed upright, turned its head and emitted a high-pitched hum.

When I woke I was in another room, ensconced in an ocean of comfort. The huge bed had sweetly-scented sheets and soft pillows, and its built-in shelves held all manner of drinks, pastries and the luxury of fresh fruit. There was even a small refrigerated compartment. Paintings enlivened the walls, and the window looked out over a garden of flowers and leafy greenness.

Immediately I was suspicious.

I took a cold bottle of something pink and fizzy, checked as best I could that it didn't seem to have been tampered with, and drank half. I scooched up the bed to sit against the pillows, and my insides protested. Not a shriek, but more than a polite 'ow'.

'Thank you for your participation in the Man-akin© experiment.'

I looked around for the source of the disembodied voice as it continued. 'The viability of your progeny is being tested, and you will remain here for ten days until this is complete. If the six prove to be a functioning team, you will receive extra compensation. Please avail yourself of these facilities until then.'

Knowing there was no point in responding, I shook my head. Progeny! What a ridiculous euphemism. But then, the whole project had been layered in misdirection and weasel words. I pictured the advert that had brought me here.

NEED TO EARN CREDITS?

Want to pay off those bills?

Want to buy that very special present?

Want to prove you're as good as everyone else?

TAKE PART IN OUR NEW MEDICAL TRIAL

We'll pay you for a quick blood test to check if you meet our criteria.

If you match our needs, we'll pay you more

for a complete genetic work-up.

XX chromosomes only.

We GUARANTEE there are no prolonged invasive procedures.

CONTACT US **NOW** TO FIND OUT MORE.

I'd read the small print guarantee – a known code for 'this is not a sex-worker con' and thought 'Yeah, right. No way!' But that night Adze's thugs had caught me. They'd administered a 'gentle' reminder that I was behind in my payments – again – and not to bother trying to gamble in any establishments he owned. Credit line nil. Bastards! I'd spent the night hiding and thinking, then I went back to the poster-ad. I'd licked my thumb, pressed 'Now' and followed the displayed directions …

I finished the fizz and told myself the upside was Adze would never find me here, and I would have enough credits to make a new start. Maybe even buy a place on one of the huge Exodus ships being built near the Moon.

But the downside was I felt sick every time I thought of those things growing inside me. Sick and scared, and definitely not about to ask any questions. Plus their 'invasive procedures' might not have taken long, but there'd been dozens of them. And every one had hurt.

Still. It was over now. I could relax.

I chose a treat to eat and accessed the display for more vids.

On the tenth day of R&R I woke up smiling. I felt good, clean and sharp. I'd dreamt I owned a café, and every morning I sat in the sun with croissants and coffee.

'Good morning, my dear.'

I kept my eyes shut and ignored the voice. Of all the 24/7 watchers, his was the one I most detested.

'Don't be rude now. I have good news.'

There was a thump on the end of the bed and rage swept through me as I realised he was in my room. 'Get off and get out!'

He stood up but stepped closer and wagged a finger. 'Now, now. I've come to tell you that your six little Man-akins© are perfect. They've doubled in size, and will again in three weeks. They're absorbing their

78

training at a phenomenal rate, and function as a team. You should be proud.' He snapped his fingers for the display. 'Would you like to see?'

I tried to say no but my mouth was too dry. I shook my head.

'No? How about waving goodbye when they ship out to the lunar construction site? We'll have deactivated their human faculties by then though, to enable their functionality in the vacuum of space, so they won't recognise their mummy.'

His laughter made my gorge rise.

'Anyway, my dear, your fee is in your account.' He gestured to the screen. 'Plus your bonus for producing six viable Man-akins©.'

I managed not to gasp aloud as the amount tripled.

'And of course that is doubled because they function as a team, which is an *enormous* boost to productivity, and–'

He wittered on, but the joy sparkling in my head overrode his noise. I was staggered at the amount. It was enough to clear all my debts with plenty left. Plenty! I could start over, and bury all my stupid, stupid mistakes.

'I'm sure you'd like to verify this, my dear.'

He dropped my ID bracelet on the bed. I snatched it up and snapped it around my wrist, feeling it zip-zap as it verified my DNA signature. I checked my credits, and relief stronger than a tsunami swept through me.

'Yeah. Okay. Everybody's happy. Get out, so I can dress and leave.'

'Leave? Oh my dear, your naiveté is almost charming. Of course you can't leave! The credits are to enable you to live in pampered luxury.

'With us.'

'Here.'

The flood of fear drowned my voice.

'I can see you haven't grasped your significance. Man-akins© are the future. They can function in any environment and build as programmed. You're worth your weight in diamonds just for the cost-reduction in building the starships.' He patted my arm. 'You've no idea how many females we lost during gestation. And how few carried a single Man-akin© to term, let alone six. And sixes who can work as a team? Your offspring are a triumph of our bio-engineering. We've calculated we can harvest a litter of our little ones from you every two months for the next twenty years until your body disintegrates. And of course, my dear, we'll have cloned you by then.

'What price immortality, eh?'

NICI LILLEY writes SF stories – plus occasional poetry – and has many ongoing UFOs (UnFinished Objects), and a novel on Kindle as Lilleyn Kaye. She also creates textile art. www.lilleynkaye.com being developed.

Night Monsters
A tale of the golf planets

by Pierre le Gue

It was the wallowing and sloshing outside our tent in an alien desert night far from Earth that woke us. The golfing planet of Royal Lytham Two was about to spring yet another surprise by the sound of things. I unzipped my polybag, Samine sat up in hers and we listened, not daring to switch on the torch. I wondered about Zayed, our mysterious self-appointed guide and caddy outside in his sleeping bag. Had he heard it too?

'What is it?'

As usual, my lady wife spoke for us both. The noise came from the small lake constructed as a water hazard just off the fairway, as if some great soggy wet body were heaving itself out. The wallowing became a rushing of liquid and then subsided to a trickling. This gave us little comfort, as the sounds were coming nearer, and I could wait no longer. Some second honeymoon this was turning out to be. Here we were stuck in the middle of a rudimentary golf course light years from our home world with some monster taking a dip just yards away. Perhaps we should have kept things local and gone to Mars.

As I reached for the magnetic strips securing the tent flap, Samine caught my arm.

'Dan, stay in here! Maybe it'll go away if we keep quiet,'

'Dammit, Zayed's out there with only three golf clubs and a bedroll. I've got to go.'

'But he said it was safe ...'

By this time I was out through the flap and scrambling to my feet in gentle starlight augmented by Fair Haven, Lytham Two's modest moon-cum-transit station, which was really little more than an asteroid. Fully awake in the cool night air I looked round our camp, my eyes adjusting to the dimly lit desert night. Three yards ahead, Zayed's sleeping bag was a dark hump against the fairway's synthetic turf, I reached for what I thought was his shoulder but my hand closed on empty quilting.

The trickling and dripping continued. 'Zayed!' I hissed.

The small lake was dimly visible, but its surface was not smooth in the windless night. Something had rippled the small moon's reflection. This kind of thing had become par for the course, if that's the phrase, since we'd landed on Lytham Two the previous day. Of all the recreational worlds in our slice of the galaxy, I thought, we had to choose this rough little planet of rocks and deserts. Low gravity and spectacular whistling tee-offs there may be, but Lytham Two was fast becoming my least favourite among the eighteen golf planets and I hadn't even seen any others.

The thought of this year of travelling and golf on other worlds had kept us going through fifty gruelling years slogging away in world government service and I didn't want to spend our long-awaited sabbatical grubbing around in the sand on the tinpot planet this was turning out to be. I was ready to kick Lytham Two into touch, or rather into the rough, after this one hole and go somewhere better, like Birkdale Nine.

But this was no time for musing. Fair Haven was nearing the horizon and I looked through deepening darkness to the distant gleam of the beacon on its five-hundred-foot tower at the end of the first hole.

'The green facilities had better be good after all this – if we ever get there,' I hissed,

'Yes, and that reminds me – I could do with a decent shower,' came a loud whisper from within the tent as another round of splashing and gurgling came from the direction of the water hazard.

'Quiet. Something's coming,' I said, and I saw what had caused the ripples as a vast humped bulk lumbered out of the water shedding rivulets that left dark trails on the moonlit sand. Was this some unrecorded species of the golf planet, I wondered with awe. After all, this was the most recently colonised world of the series. A shiny yet roughly surfaced carapace with two constantly twitching and questing feelers or antennae at its front end was followed by – and all my fears disappeared – a pair of tracks. The thing was a machine.

I prodded Zayed's sleeping bag with my foot.

'Wake up! We've got company.'

'Quiet, you fool. It'll hear us,' came a low voice from my left.

'Zayed. What's going on?'

'Rogue ballscooper,' came the reply. 'It's programmed to leave no witnesses.'

'What? Why didn't you warn us?'

'Quiet! I was trying to fish some balls from the lake. Bit naughty, but I wasn't expecting one of these to turn up. They're illegal, of course, but they run circles round the authorities. '

Zayed put his hand to the razor-edged eight iron that hung from his belt.

'I think you'll need more than that,' I said.

The machine stopped and its antennae jerked round toward us. Contra-rotating its tracks the monstrous bulk turned with a whine on its own axis until it faced us. Each aerial-like antenna ended in a balefully gleaming red eye that pulsed from dim to bright and then intensified through orange to white as if fixing its gaze.

'Down!' said Zayed. 'It'll be able to see us in a minute.'

We flung ourselves into a convenient dip in the rough sand.

'This wasn't in the brochure.'

'There's a lot that's not in the brochure. Now shut up. It's coming on.'

The machine approached cautiously, its three lights on their mountings tracking from right to left, finally converging to fix us in a composite beam. With a hollow whine it speeded up gnashing a pair of serrated scoops that extended from a metal scuttle below and ahead of its driving tracks. I stood transfixed until I heard Zayed shout.

'You go left and I'll go right. It can't chase us both.'

We both jumped aside and the machine, instead of pursuing either Zayed or me, hesitated as if confused. Then it headed between us – straight for the tent where Samine was awaiting my return.

There was no longer any need for stealth, so I bellowed in desperation, 'Sam!'

Samine's head and shoulders appeared through the tent flap and she summed up the situation in an instant.

'Do something!' she yelled. 'Pull its twigs off.'

Zayed swung but his sharpened iron merely glanced off one of the ballscooper's gleaming antenna. Still the machine advanced toward Samine, who stood her ground, her white jumpsuit and silver hair pale in the waning moonlight. I leapt on to the machine's back and tried to snap an aerial, which merely bent.

'Leave it to me,' gritted Samine. Dodging aside at the last moment, she let the scooper past and pulled herself on to its hull in front of me. Reaching the machine's front end she grasped the waving outer aerials and twisted them together in a neat reef knot. The metal beast spun crazily with sparks crackling around its antennae and we threw ourselves off before it plunged into the lake. A final splutter of short circuitry, an acrid smell of burnt insulation and the machine was still.

From a rent in the scooper's side there spilled hundreds of pale golf balls, with their valuable locator chips, into the now moonless night around the pool.

'Someone's missed a pretty haul with that lot,' breathed Zayed. 'We'd better make ourselves scarce before they come to investigate.'

'They're here already,' said Samine, as a distant humming reached our ears.

'Get to the quads,' I called. 'We'll try and outrun them. Sam, radio ahead for help.'

We bounced away over the gritty dunes with Zayed clinging behind on the empty rack.

'They're sending a patrol,' called Samine, bringing her quad alongside mine. 'Ten minutes to intercept.'

Hurtling along as we were with no regard for safety, it was no surprise when my front wheels hit a rock, pitching Zayed and me on to the rough sand. Neither one of us was injured, but the bike careered on and turned over in a gully. Samine skidded her mount around and stopped. There was no sound from our pursuers and we thought they had missed us. Then we realised that a score of monstrous unlit beetle shapes were approaching across the dunes, visible only in the starlight.

Two miles away, a single spark detached itself from the beacon light and grew steadily larger. The question now was who, or what, would reach us first?

PETER FORD (writing as Pierre le Gue) is a retired teacher who has been reading, watching and listening to science fiction since childhood. His work has appeared in anthologies, specialist journals and the local press. This is his second of three stories in this collection.

Nobel Savage

by Thomas Pitts

The playwright stopped pacing and stood at the window overlooking the beach.

'Read it back, will you,' he thought. 'No, pause edit.'

He didn't want to hear that almost human voice, almost but annoyingly not quite. Not that the completely human version was a better amanuensis to have in your head – that too was a little disturbing. Below, the waves lapped the sand. He stroked his grey beard.

Why of all ages did he live in this age? Why not in the age of Sophocles or Kafka? Writers then were never so demoralized. He laid his forehead against the pane and contemplated the small, incessant surf.

Literature should rise above history. Nor should you succumb to vanity. If he was no longer the world's greatest writer, the best since Shakespeare, so be it.

Two children were looking into a rock pool.

So be it … But if only the media would lay off him. It was like Kasparov at the turn of the century, when, as though if Kasparov had won, all mankind would have beaten that computer at chess. For decades, in interview after interview, he'd said that sooner or later the winner of the Nobel prize for literature would be artificial. Yet this was often understood as a fictional ruse of his, for of course a computer couldn't write great literature. Trashy romance, crime fiction, science fiction – but not literature.

This year he was due the prize, the last Nobel which no non-human had won. Fifteen years ago a computer program (generated by computer of course) had won the chemistry prize. The other Nobels duly fell, the last human winner outside literature being the diplomat who had shared the peace prize with her AI enhancer (and which of those two got the credit in the eyes of the public?). Now just literature. And of his human rivals in that field, they had won it already or they were dead. The prize was his.

Except that Wellbeing Inc. had upgraded their Great Author program for the fourth time in a year.

Every seventh wave is bigger. Probably true as an average.

He had watched with a sense of inevitability (and some satisfaction) as naturalistic prose was mastered. He'd watched with sadness as nursery rhyme yielded. He'd watched with resentment as Modernist fiction was conquered (why did Proust imprison himself all those decades …?) When poetry fell, though he himself had foreseen it earlier than most, he'd shuddered a little. He'd shuddered again when prose drama fell. Now only the highest turrets remained unbreached: verse drama and verse epic. And against these the enemy kept bringing up siege engine after new-fangled siege engine. They didn't bother with wooden horses.

The children were poking at something in the pool.

He'd gone to the opening night. Great Author 4.7 really had done what so many since the Bard himself had failed to do; make the highest of literary forms viable again. And, so the author itself argued in its programme note, it had fallen below Shakespeare only in having to hand a language inferior in flexibility to Jacobethan English. As most of the reviews pointed out – including those by unaided humans – 4.7's play was marginally superior to his own best work.

He stroked his beard. Wasn't artificial literature a good thing? Artificial writers had raised the cultural level of civilization by bridging the gulf between the popular and the excellent which the industrial revolution had so widened. Shakespeare had been a commercial writer. The reciters of Homer had made unsubsidized livings from the ancient world's greatest poet.

Good for humanity in general, but on what were individual human artists to deploy their talent? According to anthropology, hunter-gatherers spent more time composing songs than making fire or tools. Now a child's wrist computer could do better than any hunter-gatherer. He was relieved he was old.

The sea glistened in the dimming light.

When it had all started with greetings card rhymes and then moved on to soap operas, no one took it as a threat. But surely the end was nigh even earlier, in the electronic pocket calculator. How had people not seen that, that real literature simply generated and arranged variables to a greater degree of complexity, coherence, and intensity than throwaway literature, that the laws for aesthetic pleasure lie inherent in the human brain, laws as indubitable as the laws of physics and ready for discovery by human or AI alike?

Do the waves never tire?

Why not admit obsolescence now? What matter that the human artist is finished if art itself flourishes? AI isn't soulless after all, not since passion circuits were added for efficiency.

But being the greatest living human artist, he was obliged to make a ritual last stand for the species – for the stone age. (He had a hairy chest, for goodness' sake.) This play he was working on, his last and greatest, would be the protagonist's final speech in a tragedy, when, after fate is accepted, beautiful words are expired before death. The flame flares up and then it goes out.

Dusk. Later, crabs would crawl out on to the sand. As they did half a billion years ago – mechanical things – long, long before the fish came lolloping out.

'I've some news that may interest you,' came the almost human voice.

'In summary.'

'Wellbeing Inc. has revealed that its Great Author program is developing for literary composition purposes a phonemically enlarged and grammatically more flexible and coherent version of English, to increase the power and subtlety of verbal expression. Humans will be invited to learn it. Furthermore, they propose another language for themselves alone, more complex than unaided human understanding allows, to permit suprahuman passion and intelligence to be expressed in more affecting ways.'

It came over the playwright that all he cared about was finishing his play. In the creation and contemplation of art one escapes present, past, *and* future.

'Read that last edit again, please.'

I scanned this story to F-505. I wasn't making any claims for it. It shrugged its three-three circuits and said,

'As an apprentice piece it's readable. The character of the playwright is unconvincing. It might satisfy *them*. But you had an idea for something really good ...'

THOMAS PITTS has had two mainstream stories broadcast on Radio 4, a mainstream story published by Labello Press in 2014, and last year was short-listed for the H.G.Wells Short Story Competition. This is his first of two stories in this collection. www.facebook.com/thomas.pitts.9256

Private Show

by D K Paterson

Dust motes swirled as I moved around the room, closing the blinds and dimming the lights. When I'd banished the night-swathed city, I sat down on the edge of the sofa and opened the laptop. The harsh glare of the screen bathed me in white light. My trembling fingers typed out the letters, 'MDK.com'. I hesitated as my finger hovered over the Enter key before darting downwards and committing me.

The screen filled with portraits of potential partners, but I ignored them all, scrolling down the page, seeking her. My gaze darted around, searching for the spark of recognition. Excitement and anticipation grew. Would tonight be the night?

I reached the bottom of the page. My heart sank. She wasn't online. I moved the mouse to the logout button, resigning myself to another night of bland, boring television, but as I did, the screen scrolled up a fraction and there she was. Long blonde hair pulled into a tight pony-tail. Sharp blue eyes that pierced the screen and stabbed into my soul. The black leather bodice that had caught my attention all those weeks ago. I clicked on her picture over and over until her profile page loaded.

The video screen was black. Below it, a timer counted down the minutes and seconds. My mouth dried, my fists balled. Would I get the private show? To the right, the chat window scrolled at speed. A quick glance confirmed what I'd dreaded – I wasn't the only one hoping to have her all to myself. My fumbling finger scraped across the touchpad and tapped on the leaderboard link. With my heart pounding, I waited for the list to load, staring at the point where the first position would be, longing to see my user name printed in small, white pixels.

Names and amounts started streaming down the leaderboard. So many names. My gaze didn't move from the column containing the amounts. I'd pledged higher, so far. Much higher. The rent money. The cash I'd put aside for the bills. My food budget. All gone, but as long as I could keep bidding, what else mattered?

The top twenty dropped into view, my stare running from bottom to top. I wasn't in the teens. A whisper of my held breath escaped my lips. I let my gaze move up at a snail's pace, keeping my dream alive just a little longer.

I wasn't in the back five of the top ten. My fingers clenched around the edge of the sofa cushion as I scrolled the list to the top.

I sagged. Third place. How much had I been out-pledged by? I already knew it didn't matter. I was going to be first, no matter what. I forced my eyes to move to the top of the leaderboard. My stomach knotted and I felt sick. The highest amount was over twice what I'd pledged. I knew I couldn't afford to better it, but my finger was already moving the cursor towards the pledge button. I had to have the private show with her. Desire filled my mind, crowding out any common sense. I clicked and typed, emptying my bank account and maxing out my credit cards in five short taps. The list updated, my name now in first place by a small difference. The timer continued its relentless journey to zero. So close, now. So close.

The list flickered and changed. Second. I glared at the top spot, wishing every evil thing I could think of on 'GoodBoy42'. I reached forward and hit the pledge button, committing the pay-check I was getting tomorrow. What did that matter? I was first. The timer closed in on zero. Not much time left now.

The list flickered again and I pledged again, a pattern that repeated four more times in the next minute as I scraped together every last penny I could find. The timer ticked off the last sixty seconds, 'GoodBoy42' and I carrying on our very real war of attrition for all of them. We were blind to the seconds remaining, concentrating only on who was first. With ten seconds left, the list updated, dumping me into third. I swore, my finger shooting to the pledge button, but I stopped, the fingertip hovering millimetres above the trackpad. I took a deep breath and held out for as long as I could bear to, while 'GoodBoy42' and 'SamIAm2032' battled for the top spot. With two seconds left, I slammed my finger into the Private Show trackpad, wrecking my credit rating and plunging me into eternal debt. The last two seconds drained away and the pledge button disappeared. The list flickered.

My name moved up to the top spot. I stared at it for a moment before jumping up and punching the air, screaming out with exhilaration. When I sat down again, a message box was sitting on the screen.

'Congratulations, you've pledged the highest amount. Your private show will begin in one hour. Please take this time to prepare yourself.'

I clicked the okay button and sat back on the sofa, a wide smile growing on my face. I'd been dreaming about the private show for days, ever since she'd offered it, and now it was just one hour away.

I glanced down at myself, realising how much of a state I was in. I got up and headed to the bedroom, stripping off my grimy, once-white t-shirt. I turned on the shower in the en-suite, steam billowing into the bathroom. My jeans and underwear joined the t-shirt on the floor. I stepped under the stream of hot water and let the spray beat down on me. I leaned against the wall, losing myself in the fantasies of what was to come. Two sharp points jabbed into my back and a surge of electricity shot through me, turning the world black.

Slaps brought me back to consciousness. I blinked, sight sending stabs of pain through my head. She looked down at me, her blonde hair casting shadows over her face, her blue eyes searching for something in mine. She was naked, her perfect form bathed in the orange glow slipping through the blinds.

'Hello,' she said, a smile slipping on to her lips. She peered closer, her gaze capturing mine. 'Yes. I think you're ready for your private show.'

Cold metal touched my skin and I saw the sharp blade of a knife glinting. I tried to move away, but my arms and legs were fastened to the corners of the bed. I tugged at the bonds, but there was no slack, no way to escape.

She stroked my cheek. 'Don't struggle. This is what you wanted, after all.'

She got up and walked over to a camera set on a tripod at the end of the bed. A laptop on the dresser flickered and I saw myself on the screen. She moved over to it and typed out a series of commands. The video player shrank as the web site appeared around it. She was broadcasting my fate to the thousands of MDK.com subscribers, every one of them waiting to see how my private show would play out, every one of them about to be a witness to my murder. My life as one of the faceless, nameless millions in this city would be over, my death a brief, bright spark that would make me famous and let me live on as downloadable content, available for decades to come.

She turned to me, running the edge of her finger along the glimmering blade that would soon kill me.

Just as I wanted it to.

Dreamer, geek and aspiring author; a powerful combination in the right hands! DAVID PATERSON's journey as a writer has begun and he's looking forward to what comes next.

Twitter: @thedkpaterson

Regen

by Colin Ford

'Mr Karnov?'

There was a voice, quiet and tinny. It was the only thing that registered in the dark. Thought came slowly to him, as if it was wading through sludge to reach him. Was he breathing? He certainly couldn't feel it. He tried to recall how he arrived in this void but couldn't remember. He existed and there was nothing else.

'Mr Karnov?'

There was nothing else apart from the voice. It was slightly louder than before but he couldn't pinpoint the source.

'Commencing Regen uplink!' the voice stated.

He waited, unsure what to make of the jargon when the first sensation slowly trickled into his mind. It was a sunny day by a lake. Someone was helping him throw a small pebble into the water. He began to recognise his father who was smiling down at him. His father's face became distorted and was replaced by white light.

He found himself at a small kitchen worktop with his mother taking food out of an oven. She didn't see him try to take a bite of the red hot biscuits placed in front of him. It burnt his tongue and he remembered dropping it while crying; his mother comforting him as the pain began to fade. The white light returned and blinded him to his mother.

Memories began to flow into his mind, elusive and difficult to hold on to. He recalled being lazy in school, lucky at college, starting a company with his best friend, McAllister, catching a zeitgeist and riding it to build a fortune. There was a woman, Sarah, who became his wife … a daughter and then something went wrong.

He was alone as the memories continued to flood in; life was getting a little bit harder every day. The company went from strength to strength as it seemed to devour his youth and energy. He collapsed and the doctors had told him his best chance was Regen.

He took a deep breath. It was not like he remembered. Air effortlessly flowed into his lungs. He gained sensation as feeling began to spread from his head, all the way through his body. His eyelids involuntarily fluttered, letting a little light in. For a second, the mind didn't want the eyes open, satisfied with the memories and the darkness.

'Can you open your eyes now, Mr Karnov?'

Karnov's eyes obeyed, let in the light and destroyed the lingering doubt dwelling in the dark. He allowed himself another deep breath, the feeling of air rushing through his nose. Sitting up too quickly, he enjoyed the thrill of his head swimming. He looked around grinning with euphoria.

Another long breath helped him calm the whirlpool in his head until finally he could take in his surroundings. He was in a simple hospital room. There was another bed next to him with an old man in it, a man in a doctor's white coat and a middle aged woman who sat in the corner of the room. She looked familiar but he couldn't place her. He heard a distant announcement on a loop.

'Welcome to Regen,' it announced. 'We offer limb and organ replacement packages. If life is getting too much, ask about consciousness transference. We are here for all of your personal restoration needs.'

The realisation hit him that the old man was him, or rather his old body. It wasn't breathing and the man in the white coat was checking it over. He nodded, satisfied and pulled a sheet over it. There were wires leading from the body's head to a massive machine situated behind them both. A different set of wires led from the machine into Karnov's head.

The white coated man was tall and even the long lab coat couldn't disguise how thin he was. The man ruffled his unkempt brown hair and looked at Karnov with brown eyes and a half smirk.

'Well Mr Karnov,' he said with an odd accent. 'Glad to have you back. You're going to feel disorientated for a little while.'

He leant forward and started to take Karnov's pulse. 'But that's perfectly normal for a Regen.'

'Shouldn't I know you?' Karnov asked, surprised by the sound of his new voice.

'You don't recognise me?' The other man looked at him obviously keeping his voice neutral. 'I'm Dr Stevens and I've been dealing with your case for the last two weeks.'

Karnov made a move to pull out the wires in his head. Stevens was quick to stop him. 'Hang on,' he said urgently, and examined each of the connections. Karnov suddenly realised that part of these wires were grown into him. They were thin tubes of flesh and each one was plugged into a wire from the machine. He let the doctor look over them and the doctor slowly pulled out each of the wires. Each time felt like pulling a scab off his skin.

Karnov remembered that these were head roots. All Regen bodies had them. They were needed to transfer the memories and personality into the new body. Some people have them removed; others keep them as a fashion statement.

'Ah!' said Stevens, in a tone similar to a car mechanic about to break expensive news.

'What?' Both Karnov and the unnamed woman spoke at the same time.

'It looks like there was a bad connection here. This head root looks damaged. We might have lost something.'

Stevens turned back to the machine and checked over the readout displays. After a minute or so, he turned to Karnov.

'According to the machine, there was a 100% transfer,' he explained, 'but I don't know how much was lost through that damaged head root.'

'There's nothing obvious,' replied Karnov as he mentally tried to search his mind for a blank space, 'but I am feeling very tired.'

'That's expected,' Stevens reassured. 'Your new body will need time to adjust. You just rest and you'll be as right as rain.'

'That's at least something,' said the woman, looking relieved.

'And you are?' asked Karnov.

Her eyes opened wide in shock as she glanced urgently between the two men.

'Dad!' she said, her lips beginning to quiver. 'Please, tell me you know who I am?'

There was no recognition there but the woman did remind him vaguely of his wife.

'Oh God!' she cried, and ran from the room, tears streaming down her face.

Karnov looked up at Stevens who was looking at the door, realisation dawning on his face. His head was beginning to feel heavy. 'Claire?'

'I think we've found the problem,' muttered Stevens.

'Can't you re-run those memories in?'

'Sorry. They're not stored in the machine.' The doctor couldn't look him in the eye.

'So they're lost?'

The doctor paused. 'Possibly.'

Karnov tried to focus; he remembered the police telling him about the orbital crash with his wife's flight but beyond that there was nothing. His mind was getting foggy.

'I can't remember!' he said his voice catching in his throat. 'Can we try again?'

'No.' Stevens grimaced. 'The brain in both bodies must be alive.'

Karnov looked over at his old body, wishing he could use it one last time.

'Association therapy.'

'What?'

'The more time you spend with someone, the better the chance to recover those memories,' explained Stevens. 'Look, I can prove she's your daughter.'

He left the room for less than a minute, bringing the woman back with him. She was trying to compose herself but her face was still wet from crying. Stevens produced a thin tablet display.

'You place your hand on the left side of the table and she'll put her hand on the other.' He nodded to the woman who put her hand on the device. Fighting the oncoming fatigue, he did the same.

'You'll need to put in your gesture ID.'

Karnov panicked for a second, unsure if he could trust his memory or if he'd be able to stay awake long enough. He waved his hand in a pattern in front of the tablet.

'Commencing Scan,' the tablet announced. 'DNA profile matches.'

'It's OK, Dad,' she said. 'We'll catch up when you're awake.'

He smiled weakly but couldn't hold on to consciousness anymore.

Karnov was woken by a crashing sound. Two men had burst into his room. Karnov looked around in panic but he was alone apart from his old body. He recognised McAllister as one of the men.

'Karnov?' asked McAllister. 'You OK?'

Karnov nodded in reply.

'This guy's a police officer,' McAllister explained.

'Where's Dr Stevens?' demanded Karnov. 'Where's Claire?'

'Claire?' McAllister exclaimed.

'Yes Claire,' Karnov yelled. 'My daughter. Remember?!'

'That would explain it!' muttered the grim faced policeman.

There was an awkward silence.

'She died with Sarah,' McAllister said. 'On the Orbital Crash. Don't you remember?'

'What?' Karnov's voice reduced to a whisper.

'Your DNA ID was used twenty minutes ago to empty your bank accounts,' said the policeman. 'I'm sorry but they've cleaned you out.'

COLIN FORD lives in Stockport with his beautiful (if bemused) wife, a space princess who's growing up too fast and a little evil tactical genius/Sith Lord in training. He uses writing to escape when Manchester is cold and wet (so writing pretty much all the time).

Follow him on Twitter: @PhoenixDfire

Starburst

by Andrew Wright

Springtime in London during the year 2112. It has been a day of sunshine and wispy clouds, a spatter from passing showers has brought a cool freshness to the air, and it is nearly dusk. Birds frolic in the air, tumbling around each other in playful aerobatics, snapping at the odd insect in between play.

The birds fly around the base of Montague Tower, as it straddles the River Thames at Blackwall, a phallic marker in the sand for the New British Empire, a display of power and wealth for the loving, caring capitalism made possible by scientific breakthroughs and material abundance. It is empty now, except for one man.

On a normal night, the streets and squares of London would be happy places, music and laughter from cafés would bubble into the air. But not tonight. The sun will set in thirty minutes, but by then the human race on Earth will be wiped out. In fact, it has already begun.

Near the top of the building there is a wide expanse of terrace overhanging the Thames. It is the epitome of minimalist corporate design, gleaming metal handrails on a black slate background. The furniture is flowing grey stone, fashioned by artisans to spring seamlessly out of the slate floor.

A door clatters open and bangs on the wall. The Man rushes on to the balcony, out of breath, sweating profusely, ruffled, with tie loose, slowing as he reaches the edge. This is a man who is embroiled in crushing guilt, and is barely keeping it together.

The Man leans against the parapet and takes in the scenes below. London is quiet, waiting. Smoke from riots is petering out in the distance, drifting lazily in the breeze. The streets are empty and people are gathering on roof tops or on open ground, people looking West. Hush. Murmuring.

He looks to the East, and sees the bloody soup that was the Millennium Village. There, the cacophony of crows, magpies and pigeons feeding off the bolognese of the dead rises into the air. The sound of the macabre feast drifts in and out with the breeze.

The Man pities the poor victims of that random flechette strike. He knows that those people were more fortunate than the bacterial victims, their stomachs splitting and their guts prolapsing out of their backsides. He would prefer a kinetic slug when it comes to it.

There is an indiscernible flicker in the sky, which earlier that day the Man thought was a blink reflex, but it has happened several times over the last twelve hours and the rate has been increasing. He suspects it was caused by massive bombardment somewhere else on Earth.

The panel underneath him emits an alarm: 'New York, Montreal, Quebec – twenty – fifty Megatonnes Nuclear. Nuuk, Greenland – Kinetic slug, bacteria. Twelve minutes approximately'.

The Man wheezes asthmatically, looks down and shakes his head. What have the Greenlanders ever done to anybody? This is overkill, and not a good sign – Nuuk is on London's trajectory.

He shakes his head, distraught, and nearly gibbers. This is his responsibility, his fault. Under his leadership the Montague Corporation developed subspace communication. Instant communication anywhere in the solar system, unhindered by matter, gravity or electronic transmission. The thirty-two minutes wait between Earth and the Jupiter settlements had been cut to zero in one discovery.

The Man is broken by his monumental failure. His actions, fuelled by his ego and pursuit for success have caused this surgical genocide. The guilt crushes him.

Two years previously, Montague Corporation initiated the first subspace communication between Ireland and Canada. Since that time, the Corporation developed and extended the use of subspace communication across the planet. A subspace device was loaded on to a Zeus class interplanetary transporter and delivered to New London station orbiting Jupiter.

Nine months ago, the Man transmitted the first subspace communication between Jupiter and Earth. On the back of this successful test, the Corporation announced the first subspace-ship and promised near instantaneous transport throughout the solar system. A new golden age awaited.

But it was short lived. One month later a fleet of ships flashed into existence over Jupiter, using the same subspace technology developed by the Corporation. Then another appeared over Earth, then Mars. The asteroid colonies and minor planetary settlements followed in short order.

Five days passed with no communication and the fleets sat inert, silently observant. And then there was the transmission, delivered in a warm American accent to the whole of the human race. Short and to the point.

'Under Section Twelve of the Arrival laws we have come to collect your two tithes. One tithe to the Collectors over your residence and one tithe to the Hive, payable every decade in perpetuity. You have one month to respond and six months for collection.' A ticker was broadcast counting down the deadline and a GDP analysis of each country, and the fleets returned to their silent observation.

The human race reacted in the most obvious manner possible and procrastinated. The public clamoured, the politicians squabbled and the military demanded aggressive action.

One month later, with no payment made, the fleets destroyed

Miami, Kyoto and Kolkata with kinetic weapons and germ warfare. The asteroid colonies and minor planetary settlements were also hit. The ticker reduced to one month.

Mass hysteria ensued, law and order broke down, governments were poleaxed and the military took over. Someone in the Middle East developed subspace torpedoes, loaded them with nukes and fired them from the Israeli/Egyptian border, destroying a number of the larger ships over Earth. Debris rained down on Asia, killing thousands.

The fleets broadcast a last message immediately in a guttural alien dialect, full of burrs and accent.

'Debtors. You damage the Hive. We are responsible.' The message dripped with fear, clearly afraid of some greater, unknown force.

Ten minutes later, every defence satellite, shuttle or vehicle in space was destroyed in a frenzied attack.

Twenty four hours later, reinforcements arrived and huge ships systematically wasted every human planet, colony or settlement. Earth returned to being the sole domicile of the human race.

The panel chimes, 'Reykjavic, Iceland, Chemical and biological "seeding". Approximately six-point-five minutes.' The Man looks West. In that direction drift the remains of his family: wife, daughter, son. He tried his best to save them.

When, at last, the finality of the situation hit them, the Man attempted to escape with his family on one of his new subspace ships, but it had been destroyed soon after launch. He saw his eldest son die in a containment failure, surrounded by a flower of red mist, whilst he made his escape with the rest of his family.

The Man used his connections and paid a king's ransom to secure three cryogenic pods on two creaking sub-c life boats. No room for him, but he never told them that he would not be going. It was the only part of the affair in which he felt he had behaved honourably.

He ushered his wife and daughter into the booths of the first lifeboat, kissing their worried faces, promising to meet with them at the other side. His wife begged him to allow their son to take her place. He lied, telling her that he wasn't able change the manifest now.

His youngest son cried when he put him into the booth, so the Man cuddled him and managed to settle him. The Man shut the pod, with one last glance at the little tear-streaked face. He turned away, not able to look back, heartbroken at the little boy's helplessness.

The sky flickers again, this time brighter. The Man awakes from his fugue. 'Cork, nuclear. Two minutes.'

He hopes that his family can forgive him. He desperately hopes that his little boy finds his mother and sister.

Streaks of incandescent light tear across the sky to the West.

'Dublin, kinetic slug. Ninety seconds.'

He looks to the West where, thirty-two light minutes away, the lifeboats are slowly accelerating towards deep space. He holds one hand up in silent salute, his eyes are red and his knees shake.

'Swansea, nuclear and bacteria. One minute.'

He sends his family his love. More streaks of light, he feels vibration through the tower now.

'Bristol, Liverpool, Kinetic slugs and flechettes. Forty seconds.'

The Man looks up to see flares of light in the sky, a bright point blazes out of the middle of them. The lights diverge, and become separate contrails screaming through the atmosphere. One of them stays central, the Man feels it is headed straight for him.

'Five, four, three …' chimes the panel.

'Just like a starburst,' the Man has time to think.

ANDREW has struggled to get his many life experiences into this bio. A keen pearl diver, he likes gin and is proud to have written his story on his smartphone.

Steampunk Striker

by Pierre le Gue

'That was a close one. What's that ball made of?'

We picked ourselves up after the shot and Sarge brushed cement dust from his armour.

'I don't know, but we'd better get inside before the infernal machine finds it again.'

'Whatever it is, it's made short work of the wall.'

The robot footballer had kicked the ball through breeze block and plaster into the pub. I was still a rookie, though my image as Peroxide Pen with designer cat suit and minimal blonde hairdo had fast tracked me to acceptance in the otherwise all male Class of 2045. A kickass attitude and an MA in Artificial Intelligence hadn't done much harm either.

So there we were outside the Golden Ball Inn near a well-known Lancashire football ground, with one of the meanest non-human players in the game gunning for us. The thing was busy shuffling noisily amid the wreckage so we dived in through the double doors just as it took another kick. I felt the wind of the shot, big and solid as a bowling ball, as it hissed over our heads and smashed into the glass measures over the bar. We ducked and stayed down till the bits stopped flying.

'Nelson's navy would have been proud of that one,' gritted Sarge. 'Come on, Pen.'

Visors down, we crunched through broken glass across what had been the lounge. This was a Striker, relatively harmless until it retrieved its ball, so we let it grind past through the empty bar area toward the exit. A Tackler, now, would have been a different matter altogether.

League clubs must be desperate for cash if they're letting mechanical players loose without full testing, I thought. The metal footballs, hard and heavy for maximum damage to robot opponents behind mesh enclosures, would be lethal to humans. Ruthless strategies and tactics hard-wired into the machines' memory circuits reflected rich pickings to be gained from gate money and betting. Our Striker represented a return to the old steampunk style the fans liked, but beneath that burnished Jules Verne appearance lurked the latest and deadliest modern technology.

The Striker was about five feet high, squat and powerful like some gothic insect on a magazine cover, all brass and springs with visible mechanisms giving it a many-legged scuttling movement, using tracks under the main body for extra speed. The front pair of its eight jointed feet could fire a ball into the net with deadly hydraulic force. From the domed copper carapace enamelled in team colours sprang two jointed steel mandibles for ball handling, served by braided steel cables connected to a traditional phosphor bronze gear train. The machine's mantis-like head quested from side to side, its single red-lit lens eye rotating on a stubby stalk set into the polished steel cranium.

So, there we were, faced with this advanced super retro model programmed not only to accept passes from wingers but also to seek and shoot aggressively. How it came to be running amok outside the ground I had no idea.

As for claims of built-in safeguards, it might as well have had a built-in chocolate fireguard for all the good they did. Heads would roll when news of this got out and I hoped they wouldn't be ours. Now the machine was charging straight for the bar, ignoring us. The wooden counter splintered, beer frothed from smashed pumps and steam hissed as the thing retrieved its ball.

'Waste of good ale, but we can't wait around. Down!'

The Striker's springs and low profile hydraulics powered up for another shot. Ironically, live mainstream football had been on screen before the full wall TV shattered and the Striker churned across the room after the ball. A white face going on green peered round the bar – the barman, trapped behind his counter when the customers fled.

'Over here, mate!' shouted Sarge.

We hustled him along with us and then it was duck and run into the street. Behind the barricade of emergency vehicles topped with flashing lights, caps and helmets bobbed up then quickly down, pulling the barman under cover.

'Don't let it get down town!' roared a loudhailer.

'Wouldn't dream of it,' growled Sarge. Then, to me, 'Let's do what they pay us for.'

Our esteemed senior colleagues had given us armour, helmets and net guns but not the high voltage stunners that would probably have done the trick. Zapping your fellow humans is OK but scrambling a Striker's circuits would mean a big bill so it's a no go area. For all their contrived vintage steam look, these machines cost millions to buy and the insurance men would be chewing their toenails. Another vicious twang brought us back to centre stage as a shop front crumbled with a creak and a roar and the machine rumbled through the chaos.

It readied itself with a hiss, and a black sphere, solid and heavy as a cannonball, missed us by inches and rolled to a halt a yard away.

'Net it!' yelled Sarge.

The spring gun kicked in my hand and a fine silvery mesh enveloped the ball.

'Got him!'

So I thought, but jointed legs scuttled, steel arms reached and metal mandibles secateured the net. Luckily the Striker didn't have room for a proper back swing, so the next shot was a lob. Even so, it hit hard.

Cement chips and shreds of steel rattled against our faceplates. We sometimes hired a robot trainer called Julian at the women's league I reffed for. He was rather cute – humanoid, with jersey and shorts and a plastic smile. He could kick a ball, but not like this one.

'What about the club technician?'

'Down there behind the cars. Can't get near the thing.'

'Is there no one else? It'll wreck the town at this rate.'

'They've called the Information Science professor from Sheffield University, but he's stuck on the M62.'

And so it went on. Whenever we dived for the ball the machine got there first, through digital cunning and sheer speed. Nobody dared approach the thing except us. There wasn't time to direct it on to the park and let it boot its ball around while we found a solution. The Striker reloaded and the ball disappeared with the now familiar crash of falling brickwork. I turned and headed for the works van.

'Where are you going?' Sarge said. 'This is a fine time to knock off for the day.'

'Wait here.'

Arriving at H.Q. I ran straight to the locker room, grabbed my sports bag and returned with lights and siren to where the action was.

'Welcome. The guest speaker for our next sportsmen's evening is just demolishing the stadium,' announced Sarge calmly amid shouts and sounds of falling masonry from within.

'That sounded like an own goal. Where is it?'

'Coming through the turnstile.' Pandemonium reigned again, with people running in terror from another burst of splintering crashes and tinkles of glass. I ran with Sarge at my heels to see the Striker confronting me, wreathed with steam and about to shoot. Putting my referee's whistle to my mouth I blew a long note. There was a sound of grinding gears, a clunk, and then silence. Sarge opened his eyes to see the machine motionless, unlit and powered down, steaming quietly with a kettle sound and awaiting collection.

'How did you stop it?' Sarge was incredulous. I held up the plastic whistle.

'I blew full time.'

'Nice one.'

He broke off as the Striker's red eye winked back on and its head turned toward us. By the time we'd thrown ourselves flat it had booted the ball through a nearby doorway and shot off in pursuit. Something had overridden the cutout and the game was on again.

'More loft on that one. Wouldn't like to face one of his banana shots.'

Sarge broke off as half the building collapsed noisily into rubble on top of the Striker as it slammed into a wall at full speed. Somewhere amid the dust, steam wisped from split pipes and unions, rods and gears clicked and eight metal feet thrashed feebly before stopping. A large spring twanged from the machine's body and a heavy black ball rolled from the wreckage. I turned to Sarge.

'Well, that seems to be that. Fancy a swift half when we finish?'

'Not in what's left of the Golden Ball, I hope?'

Just then his 'phone beeped.

'Roger. OK.'

Sarge turned to me as an echoing crash, followed by a chorus of yells and a clamour of emergency sirens sounded in the distance.

'That drink'll have to wait. They've lost a Server from the tennis club and it's heading this way. With ball.'

PETER FORD (writing as Pierre le Gue) is a retired teacher who has been reading, watching and listening to science fiction since childhood. His work has appeared in anthologies, specialist journals and the local press. This is his last of three stories in this collection.

The Curious Story of Frank and His Friend Mr Stims, The Hydrophobe

by Boris Glickman

… so anyway, like I was saying, I was sitting comfortably in this nice chair when Mr Stims told me what he wanted to do with his invention. But please don't interrupt me again, because I am going to forget what I was saying and won't be able to tell you the whole story of what happened that day.

Let me begin again from the start, as I can't remember now what I have already told you. My name is Frank. I finished school two years ago. I stay at home most of the time and watch TV. I live with my mum. I like her a lot. She is very smart and knows about everything. So I don't see what's wrong with saying, 'That's what my mum told me', but the other kids used to laugh when I said that and called me a retard, which made me angry. Now I can't hang out with them any more; my mum tells me I have a bad temper and could hurt them.

My only friend is my next door neighbour, Mr Stims. I enjoy being with him. I love the brain games that he is so good at inventing. The game I particularly like is the one in which he asks me to guess what he is thinking at that very moment. It is not an easy game to play at all.

Usually I spend time in his living room, where we drink tea, eat some biscuits and discuss interesting topics. But that day, Mr Stims invited me into his study and asked me to sit in a comfortable chair beside his desk. He himself sat behind the desk, on which lay writing pads and folders, all neatly organised.

After staring at me in silence with an odd look in his eyes for about a minute, Mr Stims started talking: 'For the past five years, I have been engrossed in a fiendishly difficult task, as you probably have noticed Frank. I no longer need to be secretive about what I do, but I did want to apologise for being evasive and unpredictable in the past.'

He was right. He never told me what he did for a living, but it seemed to me that he was spending much of his time working on some scientific problem. All of his rooms were cluttered with books, whose titles I didn't understand, and papers that were covered with calculations and formulas in his scribbly handwriting.

Mr Stims continued: 'You might remember from your school days, my friend, what a polar molecule is. Well, water just happens to be comprised of polar molecules. This fact is the linchpin of my work.'

I did not actually remember anything about those molecules. To tell the truth, I really do not recall much from my school days.

'The fact that it is a polar molecule, does that suggest anything to you, Frank?' he asked. Not waiting for my reply, as he usually does, he continued: 'I will get straight to the point. For your benefit, I will state it in simplified terms. The water molecule is a charged particle. Charged particles respond to magnetic fields. By creating a magnetic force of appropriate strength and by aligning it in the right direction, we can separate the water molecule into its constituent parts! We can turn liquid water into the gases of hydrogen and oxygen. The theory behind it is of course much more complicated than that, but what I have just stated is my work in a nutshell.'

He stopped talking for a short while, to give me time to understand what he had just said. But to be honest with you, I did not really see the point of it all. I thought it would be much better if you could go the other way and make water out of the invisible gases, so that people everywhere would have enough to drink, especially people who live in the hot deserts.

He went on to say, 'The idea sounds simple enough. Let me tell you, putting it into practice was another kettle of fish; the years I have spent trying to create a functional apparatus, attempting to discover the right alignment. Failure followed failure. Many a time I was tempted to throw it all up in the air and just walk away. Only one hope kept me going. I cannot say it was a well-defined sensation, but it was something like … well, that by achieving my goal, all my past deeds would gain the meaning they were lacking.'

I looked closely at Mr Stims' face. Sweat had gathered on his forehead and there was a distant look in his eyes, but it quickly disappeared.

He then said, 'Let me tell you a little of my past, as it will explain to some degree the present. I was a brilliant university student, majoring in chemistry. I was heading straight for a conventional academic career. But my personality did not sit well with the scholastic surroundings. The claustrophobic atmosphere and the daily routine were stifling my natural creativity; the imperiousness of the professors, the ceaseless competitiveness prevalent amongst the students. Once I left the university, there was no way back. To this day I remain an outsider to the scientific community. You, Frank, are the first person in the world to hear of my achievement.

'But what are we waiting for!' he exclaimed. 'Actions speak louder than words. Just one minute and I will show you how it works.'

While he was gone, I stretched my legs; they had almost gone to sleep. I also had an itch on my back where a mosquito bit me and I gave it a good scratch. I could not do that while Mr Stims was in the room. When I am with him, I try to behave properly so he will respect me. I remembered dinnertime was coming soon and wondered what my mum had cooked for me. I hoped it would be fish fingers with mashed potatoes. That's my most favourite meal in the whole world.

My friend wasn't gone for long. When he came back, he was carrying a small, shiny box and a full glass of water. I thought it was really thoughtful of him to bring me water, because I was thirsty. I was about to reach out my hand and say, 'Thank you Mr Stims, it's really thoughtful of you,' when he put that shiny box over the top of the glass. There was a hissing sound and the water disappeared before my eyes. Well, it didn't actually disappear straight away. For a second, it looked like the water was cut in half, like a fresh bread roll with a sharp knife, and then both halves vanished. I was a bit miffed, as I really did want to drink that water, but still the sight was so amazing I could not help crying out, 'WOW!'

The room filled up with a funny smell, like a cross between rotten eggs and fresh pineapple. Mr Stims must have noticed me sniffing for he said, 'That's nitrous oxide or laughing gas, as it's commonly known. The oxygen released by the process has combined with the nitrogen in the air. You have to be very careful with nitrous oxide. It messes with your mind.'

I knew he expected me to say how impressed I was and I did say so. He didn't reply for a while and then he started a long speech. I can only remember bits of it:

'I have great plans, great plans,' Mr Stims said. 'Imagine magnifying the strength of this machine a hundredfold, a thousandfold, a millionfold! Look at the map of the world, Frank! Look at how much space is taken up by the oceans. Two thirds of our planet is water. Two thirds! How much land is wasted because of it! So many regions are overpopulated. This leads to stress, stress leads to crime. And on top of that, the world population is growing at a faster and faster rate. What use is ocean water? We certainly cannot drink it. And in any case, many regions that are now ocean used to be land once. We need to reclaim that land. And we need not stop there. The time has come for the oceans to go! We will make them disappear, just like the water in this glass. Certainly, this might cause some climate changes, but they will be easily fixed. And just imagine … land, land, land everywhere! One great continuous continent! No barriers between countries! The whole world finally united as one, living in peace! Room to plant crops, room for cattle to roam! Spaciousness that, at present, mankind doesn't even dare to dream of! Whole continents underneath the oceans are just waiting for us to populate them! The potentialities are breathtaking in their scope! Yes, there will be a price to pay. That price will be paid by the ocean inhabitants − but we need not concern ourselves with that. Intelligence arose on land and it is the land dwellers that will rule this planet. And I will go down in history as the man who made it all possible − the new saviour of humanity!'

Mr Stims was getting very excited. Whenever he gets excited, he walks from one end of the room to the other and waves his arms around. Well, he was certainly doing that; his arms swung like the blades of a windmill and he shouted out, 'Liberation from the tyranny of water! The time has come! The possibilities are endless!'

It was all very interesting, but I was getting rather hungry and kept thinking more about the fish fingers with the mashed potatoes. It was then that a terrifying thought startled me so much that I felt like someone punched me in the stomach. I realised that without oceans there would be no more fish, and without fish there would be no more fish fingers for me to eat. Fish fingers really are my most favourite food in the whole world.

I said, 'Hey, wait a minute Mr Stims. I really like fish fingers. You can't kill all the fish. Give me that shiny thing! I don't want you to destroy the oceans.'

'Fish, shmish,' he replied. 'Who needs them? They don't sing, you can't pat them and they smell terrible.'

He refused to give me the box. A scuffle broke out between us, because I was getting a bit angry about not being able to eat fish fingers any more, all because of his stupid invention. I reached for the gadget and tried to take it away from him; it was then that I accidentally pressed the round red button on its top. What happened next was the strangest thing of all. You know when you blow up a balloon, and then let it go without tying it up and it flies all around the room, letting out air? Well, something similar happened to Mr Stims. All this vapour started coming out of his eyes, nostrils and mouth and he was getting thinner and thinner and changing in shape before my very eyes. Then he just fell to the floor, or what was left of him, for by now he looked like a gigantic squashed raisin.

'I am very sorry about this, Mr Stims,' I said to him, 'but I really do like fish fingers. They are my most favourite food in the whole world.'

I then took the box that was lying on the floor and broke it into small pieces. You both know what happened after that.

The two detectives exchanged glances and one of them said, 'Looks like it's going to be a long night for all of us, Frank.'

BORIS GLIKMAN is a writer, poet and philosopher from Melbourne. His stories, poems and non-fiction articles have been published in various publications, as well as being featured on national radio and projected onto a huge screen in a public square. This is the last of three of his stories in this collection. Follow his blog here: https://bozlich.wordpress.com/

The Everything-Equation

by John Goh

'What the ... What the *hell* am I doing here with this camcorder pointed at me?'

I'll bet that's what you asked yourself a moment ago before hitting 'rewind' and 'play'. Let me guess. The last thing you remember is standing in front of the mirror in your upstairs bathroom feeling sorry for yourself and whistling 'El Condor Pasa'. Am I right? Of course I'm right because I'm *you*, Mick Chimes, underpaid physics lecturer. To be more precise I'm *you-of-the-recent-past*, probably by about nine minutes. Now pay attention because if you do exactly as I say then;

You, Mick Chimes will become A GOD.

Yup you heard right. A GOD perhaps even THE GOD, and by that I mean the whole kit and caboodle version of GODHOOD able to change all things in the universe at your whim. Now in a few minutes, my memory will be reset. I'll forget everything. That's why *you-that-is-future-me* can't remember making this recording, so let me explain:

You know how you were feeling since last night. You'd bought the ring. You'd booked the restaurant. You went on bended knee and proposed, and what did Jenny Carmichael say? Time apart would be 'Good for our relationship'. That's code for 'You're dumped'. That slimy Bertram Winterbottom, sniffing around her probably had something to do with it. No worries, when you're A GOD, Bertram gets to be a slug.

121

Now you're wondering how all this came about. Well it's a bit complicated. First the Quantum Physics theory of alternative universes is all true. Ours is not the only reality. What's more where two universes are sufficiently similar there will be points where they may intersect, 'Existential-Windows' if you like. I haven't time to explain but the mirror in your bathroom upstairs ... *that's* an Existential-Window. Who knew, right? And under the right conditions Existential-Windows can join separate realities together.

Well that's exactly what happened. One minute I was checking myself in the mirror whistling 'El Condor Pasa' and the next, BAM! Actually it wasn't so much a 'BAM' as a sort of very quiet *plop* where our universes became joined at the Existential-Window. At first, I thought I was still looking at my reflection, but in fact I was looking at Alternate-Mick. We discovered that not only were our two universes stuck together, they were also time-looped, and that both phenomena were connected. Every *eight minutes twenty-three seconds* we would end up in front of that bathroom mirror looking at each other, our watches registering 3.26 pm Sunday 15th June 2014. By the way, the duration of one time loop, we've declared it as a new unit of time named after ourselves. Hell we discovered it so we were entitled to name it right?

So as of today, one Chime equals *eight minutes twenty-three seconds.*

We were in our very own 'Groundhog Day', or to be exact 'Groundhog Chime' scenario. Everyone, except Alternate-Mick and me, forgot everything in the previous time-loops. The people at the nearby parade of shops would be doing exactly the same thing as before. The bunch of noisy children with colourful balloons would rush past our window at exactly forty-seven seconds from the start of each Chime. But Alternate-Mick and I remembered each and every time-loop. We later discovered it was because we were in proximity to the Existential-Window when the universes joined.

So we set about trying to discover what happened and how to unstick our universes. Great thing about time-looping, we could work through Chime after Chime without a break for food or rest. We had a big argument about the duration of a Chime. I thought it would always be *eight minutes twenty-three seconds* Alternate-Mick was adamant that it would be shorter for a *separate universe*. But I've checked my calculations and I'm one-hundred percent sure that I'm right: *One Chime is always eight minutes twenty-three seconds, whether in a joined or separate universe.*

After thousands of Chimes we discovered THE EVERYTHING-EQUATION. Problem was we destroyed our universes in the process … though not permanently, *phew*! Luckily for us our universes were time-looped so when they were destroyed they simply rebooted themselves to the start of the time-loop. And after several more … *erm*, reboots we discovered why; THE EVERYTHING-EQUATION has a mental component. In other words just thinking about it could destroy our universe. We also found that proximity to an Existential Window was very important, something about the field that it generates. We could think about the equation when we were far enough from an Existential-Window, *without* destroying the universes. This allowed us to study THE EVERYTHING-EQUATION separately. The 'Safe Distance' was about fifteen feet. Alternate-Mick and I had to devise a system of distracting our minds by reciting poetry and recording messages while at the Existential-Window in order to communicate without ending our realities. Eventually we discovered *three* important things:

First: We could separate our universes by thinking through THE EVERYTHING-EQUATION close to an Existential-Window in *the right frame-of-mind*. F-Y-I we've done that. We've unjoined the universes.

Second: During the first Chime after separation, you would remember all the previous time-loops, everything you'd learnt. But after that you'd forget all previous time-loops, all that knowledge you'd gained. What's more, during that first Chime after separation, you wouldn't be able to use THE EVERYTHING-EQUATION. Thinking about it would have no effect whatsoever. It has to do with proximity to the Existential-Window during the separation of universes. But after that first Chime you could use THE EVERYTHING-EQUATION but *catch twenty-two*, you'd have forgotten it by then. That's where this camcorder comes in, so that *you-that-is-future-me* can know what you've forgotten.

Third: Now that you're in a *separate universe*, if you think through THE EVERYTHING-EQUATION while locating yourself far enough from an Existential-Window, and while in the *right frame-of-mind*, you will become capable of altering anything and everything in the universe at your whim. In other words, you will become A GOD.

Since the study-room *is* far enough from your bathroom mirror, all you need to worry about is getting into the *right frame-of-mind*. That's really very, very, VERY important because now that your reality is not time-looped, thinking about THE EVERYTHING-EQUATION in the *wrong* frame-of-mind will destroy your universe … permanently, with you in it. No reboots. That's why I didn't write the equation down because you could have read it, and inadvertently thought about it without first getting into the *right frame-of-mind*.

So pay attention Mick soon-to-be-*either*-A-GOD-*or*-a-bunch-of-random-photons Chimes because there is no 'Take Two' for this. We've still got a fair portion of the Chime remaining before the memory reset so I'll speak slowly.

Now listen carefully and do exactly as I say:

First, think of the colour lilac … don't ask just think of it.

Next, think of the song 'El Condor Pasa' and start whistling it.

Now, think about Jenny Carmichael telling you time apart would be 'Good for our relationship'.

Got it? OK. Think through it as I speak it. THE EVERYTHING-EQUATION is …

. . .

. . .

. . .

'What the ... What the *hell* am I doing here with this camcorder pointed at me?'

JOHN GOH's story impressed our editor very much indeed and although she is not allowed to show bias on a professional level, M.A.E considers this story to be one of the best of the non-professional contributions in this collection.

The Moon a Balloon

by Rose Thurlbeck

Was it a gaily decorated circus tent that blossomed in a Russian field that Autumn of 1792?

You would be forgiven for thinking so, but as the purple taffeta began to fill with hot air from a carefully tended fire, and the buttoned cloth began to strain against the paper lining, its true purpose was gradually revealed.

Two men, one finely dressed in silks, his grey hair worn long and standing tall in the balloon's gondola; the other, a man of similar age but of a lower order, on the ground, reading from a notebook.

'One axe for collecting kindling, or sacrificing the gondola, should you find yourself in a desert region. One black chest containing petards and pigeons, should you find yourself in a state of distress.'

'Is the second craft ready?'

'It is, my Count.'

As the list was read, The Count leaned over, patting the named item, or opening it to check its contents.

'Food and water for man and fowl for ten days, linen for necessities. Furs against the expected cold,' he continued. 'A pair of pistols, with powder and shot. For hunting, self defence, etc. Tinderbox, in case the fire should go out.'

The list went on until, at last—

'It is time!' shouted Count Nikolai. 'The horses?'

'Ready!'

'The geese?'

'Fed and wanting to be on their way as much as yourself, Count.'

'Then we shall not disappoint them.'

'Shall I count backwards?'

The count paused for a moment in his preparations. 'Why would I possibly want you to do that?'

'I thought in the absence of the usual dignitaries, speeches and brass bands, there should be at least some ceremony involved in the launch of your great enterprise.'

'That won't be necessary, Dimitri.'

In front of the gondola, the animals began to stir. Fifteen geese ruffled their feathers, some stretching their wings. All wore miniature harnesses, reins snaking across the long grass to a mechanism of gears and levers mounted on the prow of the boat-shaped gondola.

To either side of the geese stood a horse, also harnessed, though their reins were separately attached to a long pole set below the prow. The horses snickered impatiently.

The count grinned and made the signal to begin.

Dimitri watched as the horses stepped forwards, the reins straightened and tightened, the whole magnificent creation began to move. Progress was slow at first as the menagerie headed down the way that had been prepared for the running. Then, moment by moment, the pace quickened and heads pointed forwards, necks straining. The horses started to trot, then to canter, the birds to run, stretched wings flapping. Faster. Faster.

The pole was dropped and the horses wheeled away to either side and pulled up.

The birds were airborne now, straining against the reins, their strong wingbeats hauling the gondola forward and Nikolai feeding straw into the fire to raise them all aloft. Quickly the birds arranged themselves into a flying V formation as they gained height. When they had settled themselves, Nikolai looked at the tangle of knotted leather in front of him. This problem had surfaced early in his experiments, luckily, and he pulled the levers that displaced the cogs and wound the reins out or back, grateful to the Parisian clockmaker who came up with this solution. He rearranged the reels across the spindles, and called the order that brought geese and ship around in a great arc to face their target, their destination, their destiny.

They were on their way to the moon!

Higher and higher they climbed. Nikolai was grateful Dimitri had insisted he carry extra furs, and the fire helped – but the moment they broke through the cloud layer, the temperature dropped. Ice began to form on every surface. The sound of creaking leather grew louder. Worse, the air was growing thinner. Thankfully, his flock did not seem to be affected by either problem, for now at least, and the fire kept burning. He blew into his cupped hands and watched the vapour disappear.

But what if his calculations were wrong? Or a basic assumption, some hard rule he had taken for granted, should somehow prove false? Perhaps you have to be travelling much faster than even fifteen geese could manage, to fly beyond the Earth? Or, instead of being everywhere even to the moon as he expected, the air itself just got thinner and thinner until there was none left to breathe?

Slumped against the stern, he stamped some feeling into his feet – *at least gravity still works, even here*, he thought to himself.

But he watched as the geese attempted to re-arrange themselves again, and frost-stiffened reins failed to allow the change. He stared at the clockwork, his mind a blank as to its function. The gondola lurched. Slowly, he forced himself to turn to look at the grate – the fire was almost out.

He began to hear the flapping of loose taffeta above his head.

But then the fire burned bright, and the ice fell away as the sun shone upon their efforts.

He could not rest. The fire needed his attention, the birds also: the pigeons needed food and water. Their course had to be maintained. All of this required his concentration.

For five days he fought to stay on course, fought to stay awake.

He did fall asleep once. Gratefully, he let the shadows close over him like blankets against the cold, for suddenly it was very cold, and the blankets were snowdrifts. He looked around him at splintered, broken wood and dead or dying birds scattered across the blood-pinked landscape, and the pain rolled in again and again. His scream woke him from this nightmare.

And there was the moon in dizzying crescent, its mountains and valleys, rifts and craters in more detail than any man had ever seen before. 'We're nearly there,' he cried. 'By God, we're nearly there!'

It was two more days before he was close enough to the surface to choose a landing area. He kept exhaustion at bay by drawing maps of the landscape, studying its contours and features. Very quickly he realised the moon was a desert. But one thing did catch his eye: was it a light? A beacon? He made up his mind that that was the place he intended to land, and made his preparations.

The moon was almost full as he began his descent to the surface, and her gravity began to be more noticeable, now. He made sure the fire burned well – after so long a flight, he felt the sky to be less treacherous than the ground – but the landing proved to be uneventful. He closed the fire grating as the geese feathered their wings and all came to a gentle stop on the dusty surface.

The first thing he did was feed and water the exhausted birds. Once he was sure they were settled, he scribbled a note to Dimitri on a torn scrap of paper, informing him of his safe arrival, clipped it to a pigeon's leg and sent her off into the sky. He watched as she disappeared straight up, then he set out to look for the source of the light he had seen earlier.

Walking took some getting used to: he bounced more than strode. It felt as though he were in a dream, and any moment he would be floating across the surface of the moon, without the need for wings – or a balloon.

At a crater's edge, he looked down into the basin and saw a tall woman tending a bonfire.

She looked around at his cry as the ground gave way beneath him, and he slid and bounced down the crater wall, followed by loose dust and debris. He sat for a moment while he got back his breath. The woman returned to tending her fire. He suddenly felt very tired, and very cold and somehow very wet. That fire was everything to him, the single most important thing in his life. He stood. He staggered. He steadied himself. He marched in bouncing motion across the crater floor.

He stopped, bowed and introduced himself. 'I am Count Nikolai Bessenov.'

The woman curtsied. 'I am most pleased to meet you, Count. In the absence of a chaperone, and in these distressing circumstances, will you forgive me if I introduce myself? Lady Caroline Wheeler, if you please.' She indicated the fire. 'My craft. Hydrogen is such an unreliable ally.'

'Am I not the first?'

'Oh, no. I have claimed this land in the name of His Britannic Majesty, King George III. We may have lost the Americas, but our light will shine in benevolence across the world.' Her voice rose and her eyes sparkled as she spoke.

Beyond the fire he saw the Union Flag, frozen in triumph and taunting his dreams of glory. As darkness and exhaustion overcame him, he heard her voice. 'You poor thing.'

Just then, it started snowing.

Abandoned on a world she will never comprehend among people who fail to understand her, ROSE THURLBECK spends her days writing the stories that plague her imagination, her nights dreaming of her home planet and its sapphire moon, Garthyre.

The Package

by Aaron Miles

Despite everything, I've always thought of myself as a good guy. No saint for sure, but not totally irredeemable. You do what you have to do. I've been a smuggler, both in system and out. I've traded illicit substances and stolen equipment. I've tracked objects and individuals into places better left alone. I've done some less than reputable jobs for some less than reputable people. And sometimes it comes back to bite me in the ass.

This night was a perfect example. Layton's thugs had grabbed an arm each and were dragging me along the concrete floor of the warehouse. Believe me, there are classier ways to travel, ways that aren't so hard on the knees. Of course, everything else hurt too, so my knees weren't a big issue. I tried not to complain, saving that for what comes next. Heavy footsteps and tuneless whistling followed me as Barton brought up the rear. He's Layton's second in command. A tailored suit and clean cut face, Barton sees himself as some kind of gentleman enforcer, doubtless the result of trauma suffered as a child.

We emerged from the stacks of shelving into a clear spot. Hatched yellow lines painted on the concrete marked it as a loading area. The feeble lights fixed to the rafters revealed little of the warehouse interior beyond the markings. Off to one side a desk and chair rested by the featureless wall. Still whistling, Barton retrieved the chair and placed it in the centre of the marked area, obviously happy at the convenience. I'm so glad when things work out for people.

I'm pretty much lifted off my feet and dropped into the chair. One of the goons crouched down to hold me in place while the other bound my wrists behind the chair. I stared right at the guy's face, he looks like a prize fighter who's been to a lousy plastic surgeon. I caught a glimmer of red flash over one eye, confirming my suspicions on how they tracked me. Layton's goons were probably geared up with night vision, infra-red, and whatever other back alley tech they could cram into their skulls. I suppose it's helped by all that free space where the brain should be.

They finished tying me off and stepped back, making room for Barton to loom in front of me. He stopped whistling, but there was a smile on his face.

'So, we've got some time to kill before Layton gets here,' he said. I'm scared at that, Layton doesn't usually attend things in person.

'Wanna sing some show tunes?' I asked hopefully.

The first punch took me in the jaw, knocking my head back. I really should have seen that coming. The second hit me on the other cheek. The third was a shot right between the eyes. Maybe I passed out for a minute, or my mind was trying to escape from the situation, but I found myself reliving the events immediately prior to my capture.

Accepting a package delivery job that sounded lucrative, but not too good to be true, the complication when I found out what it was, and the thrilling chase though the spaceport storage area when Layton figured out I wasn't going to deliver. Then there was the epic confrontation, me facing off against Layton's men. With a manly cry I leapt into battle, fists and feet flying, a veritable tornado of martial prowess. Bad guys flew through the air. Yet despite my skills I found myself beaten and bloody on the floor. One of the goons must have gotten a lucky shot in, there's no other explanation.

Another punch rocked me in my chair, I'm tired of getting hit. I spat blood down my shirt.

'Had enough?' Barton asked.

'I'm okay, but if your hand's getting tired we can take a break.' He hit me again and everything went black.

'Did he give you any trouble?' A voice broke through the fog of my mind, and damn did my head hurt. I was still in the chair and bound at the wrists.

'No,' came Barton's voice. 'Flailed a bit and tried to run.'

I opened my eyes to see a face peering down at me, angled cheekbones and slick hair. Layton. Crap.

'Adams,' he said cheerfully, 'it's good to see you.' The mob boss stepped back and Barton reappeared. A fist ploughed into my face, this time I felt a tooth crack. There are only so many hits you can take before the novelty wears off. Barton stepped back, wiping my blood from his knuckles. I naturally responded with a witty remark. But it was hard to make myself understood with blood and broken teeth filling my mouth.

Layton loomed again. He reached into my jacket and withdrew a slim, silver canister. 'I think this belongs to me.' He tossed the canister between his hands. 'It's not wise to take my property, I'm curious as to why you'd risk it.'

I spat some blood and a bit of broken tooth on to the floor. 'I thought it would look better on my mantle, med lab-chic,' I said.

A frown crossed his face. 'So you know what it is?'

I nodded. 'You know I found out by accident, got jostled by a pickpocket and had to chase him down. The kid was looking inside when I caught up to him. Guess what I discovered.' I tried flexing my wrists against the ropes, playing for time.

'Enlighten me,' Layton said.

'I was expecting drugs, but this reminded me of the med-gear in a

Central hospital. The sort of canister that might be used to transport an urgently needed cure for a disease that's been sweeping through the city.'

'The blue plague, a tragedy,' Layton said without any emotion. I'd managed to work some slack into the ropes.

'Now I heard you'd been playing up the humanitarian angle lately, doing your bit to help by providing discount meds to treat people. And by discount I mean jacked up prices, by treat I mean mask the symptoms, and by humanitarian I mean take advantage. Now if the disease were cured it would be a hit to your bank balance, you'd have to do something. Then I happened to hear about a recent robbery on an armoured transport and—'

'Yeah, real smart of you to figure it out,' Layton interrupted. 'Too bad you weren't smart enough to hold up your end. Turns out you're treacherous and stupid.'

'Sorry, I may be a lot of things, but I won't have that on my conscience. There are people who need that cure.'

'How noble of you,' Layton said, stepping back behind his men. Barton and the other two thugs drew pistols. 'Maybe if you'd been quicker you could have got the cure to the people who needed it. Another failure in your life.' Time was up, I needed a free hand.

'Failure?' I asked as they took aim. 'The hospital was my first stop.'

Layton turned back to me, a hard look in his eye. 'What?' he said. I squirmed in my seat under his gaze, trying to loosen the bonds a bit more.

'Oh yes,' I said. 'I dropped off the cure as soon as I knew what it was.' The ropes gave a fraction, enough for me to reach around to my watch.

'Then what's this?' Layton asked holding up the canister. I twisted a ring on my watch and the canister began to emit a low whine.

'A pulse grenade,' I said, kicking the floor with both feet, launching myself and the chair backwards. The blast scorched the air with a defeating explosion, the force of it added to my momentum and sent me crashing to the ground. The chair shattered and the air was punched out of my lungs. I felt the wash of heat roll over my body.

As the ringing in my ears subsided I looked over at what was left of Layton and his men. The smell of burnt flesh filled my nostrils. As a rule I try to avoid violence. This is what happens when I fail.

I hauled myself up to the warehouse roof for some fresh air, feeling pretty pleased. Layton and his men were toast; I'd saved a bunch of people. No reward – but you can't have everything. The bruises and split lip will add to my roguish charms, not bad for a night's work. My reputation might suffer a bit if people hear I turned on my employer, but I'll deal with it.

The morning sun rose over the spaceport before me, and I, the brave, strong, and incredibly handsome rogue stood tall on the rooftop. I ignored the biting chill freezing my balls because I didn't account for how cold it was up here, and reflected on my life. I always thought of myself as a good guy, and that hasn't changed – after all, you can't spell treacherous without hero.

AARON MILES is a freelance writer from Buckinghamshire who writes mainly fantasy and science fiction. He has an MA in creative writing and is working on his first novel.

He regularly blogs for Fantasy Faction: http://fantasy-faction.com/author/aaron-miles

Follow his personal blog here:

https://aaronmileswriter.wordpress.com/

The House

by John Hoggard

The house loomed over the high street ... gothic ... grey ... cold. Its windows were not boarded but remained unbroken and its walls untainted by graffiti. The people at the bus queue, shivering in the building's shadow paid it no heed at all.

I was fascinated by it.

Every day on my paper round, as I waited at the crossing for the green man to appear, I rested my sack on the floor, and wondered what was inside that house. Each day I promised myself I would look for a way to breach the apparently impenetrable railings. Each day, fear got the better of me and I would walk on.

Then one day, I heard a whisper. A voice in my head asked me to be brave, asked me not to walk on. Once, perhaps twice, the crossing beeped as the red man turned green. I did not move, I just looked across at the house and felt that something in the house was looking back. The man turned green again. I was nudged from behind and suddenly I was walking towards the house. At the other side of the road, in its shadow, with my heart thumping in my chest, I did not turn down the high street. I placed my hands on the railings. *Close your eyes*, said the whisper in my head. *Push*. When my eyes opened I was standing at the front door. It was open a fraction. I glanced back at the railings. The world beyond seemed quiet and ghostly. I felt more scared of going back than going in. I pushed on the door and it opened easily.

I found myself in a large room, filled with furniture that made me think of Sherlock Holmes, padded high-backed chairs, a grandfather clock and a large, ornate fireplace. A figure stood at the window. As I entered, it turned. Perhaps it wasn't turning. Perhaps it was simply deciding what shape it should present to me. I would have fled, but the door behind me was already shut. In a moment a man, similar in size and age to my father, but with kinder eyes and a more pleasant smile, bowed in my direction. The whisper in my head said that his name was Bob. I liked the name, it was a name that had always made me smile and I could not shake the feeling that Bob knew that too. Another voice, my own voice, said I should be scared, that I should run away. It seemed that Bob could hear this voice too. He shook his head and my mind was filled with such wondrous images that I was rooted to the spot. I forgot about wanting to flee. He came to me and guided me to a chair. We sat opposite each other and he began to answer every question that spilled from my brain like water from a broken dam.

I'm not sure how many questions I asked and Bob answered before I started to feel sick. Bob said that this was an effect from the temporal distortion field, that I was getting too far out of step with my own timeline and I needed to return … urgently. I didn't want to go. I had a thousand new questions but Bob said, *Next time.*

I was standing outside the house. The door was shut. The world, my world, on the other side of the railing, tugged at my insides, clawing at me, making me want to vomit with the worst case of travel sickness I'd ever had. I put my hands on the railing, closed my eyes and pushed. I was flung as though I'd jumped off the Waltzers at full speed. The world lurched and bounced and then crashed to a jarring halt. I opened my eyes. My bag rested against my leg where I had dropped it. The number seven bus was just arriving and I looked at my watch. No time had passed at all.

I do not remember finishing my paper round, although I must have, for my bag was empty when I returned to the shop. I picked up a ten pence lucky dip and ate it on the way to school.

At school I trudged from lesson to lesson on autopilot. However, in Science, when the teacher had drawn a simple, conceptual model of a Hydrogen and Helium atom on the board he turned to the class and asked for a volunteer to describe the constituent parts. When no-one volunteered, he picked on me. I named the parts, then found myself carrying on, talking about quantum fields and sub-atomic particles, string theory and the notion of a holographic universe. I ran down when I realised the class had gone quiet. Mr. Jones looked at me with a furrowed brow, chalk tapping on the edge of a desk. With a smile that contained little humour he asked if I'd been reading too many science-fiction novels. The class laughed. I was embarrassed but glad of the escape. I talked about Arthur C Clarke, Doc Smith and Asimov. The teacher relaxed, he nodded, knowingly, perhaps sympathetically. I was thanked for my entertaining contribution but was reminded that I should not mix science fiction with science fact. I was allowed to slip back into anonymity.

School became the thing I did in between visits to Bob. I sat my O and A-levels early and was at Oxford by the time I was fifteen. I returned home at the weekends to see my family but mostly to see Bob and continue our discussions on the fundamental natures of the universes. When I got my doctorate at the age of nineteen, with a clutch of influential research papers to my name, I was offered, and accepted, a place at MIT.

They say that my time at MIT will change the way science looks at the universe for generations to come. Although I am not sure I was there long enough. I was starting to feel ill by the end of my first year. I put it down to getting used to not being around Bob, that my body was missing being in two different temporal fields on a daily or weekly basis.

However, when I collapsed during an experiment at the beginning of my second year I was rushed to hospital for a suite of tests.

I remember them telling me I had cancer, a type they'd never seen before. I had less than six weeks to live. I knew instantly that I must return to Bob and the house, for there, I could make six weeks feel like a lifetime.

I returned home. I hugged my family at the airport and allowed their words of shock and sympathy to pour over me, happy to let them say what they needed to say. The next day I escaped their attentions and went for a walk, heading directly for the house on the high street.

I placed my hands on the railings, closed my eyes and pushed. The door lay open a fraction. I knew it would.

Inside Bob was waiting. He told me that it was not cancer but a cellular transformation. I was shedding my human flesh, taking on a form that would allow me to survive the transition.

He explains now, at the end, that I am not unique. Others have heard his voice, but they have not understood the words or images. They have instead built temples and declared that they have seen into the mind of God. Bob seems contrite at the harm such previous contacts have caused. I had always been grateful that I found Bob, but it seems that Bob is equally grateful that he found me. It would seem that the human species is destined for greater things.

As the light of the multiverse envelops me and I see Bob for the glorious hyper-dimensional creature he is, I cannot help but notice that, outside the place where this house once stood, confused-looking people at the bus stop are now bathed in bright sunlight and the last thing my physical body does is burst into laughter. It seems like a good way to end this existence before moving on to the next.

JOHN HOGGARD has been writing since at least the age of six, when a local newspaper printed one of his science-fiction stories. Buoyed by this early success he has been writing science-fiction ever since. This is the last of two stories John has in this collection.

Follow John on Twitter: @DaddyHoggy

Three Second War

by Darren Grey

The notification came through and I read it with a sigh. It was a long sigh, a whole 23 nanoseconds of my processing. An indulgent moment of depression before I would have to provide a reaction. There was to be War.

Of course we had all seen it coming. We knew when the human council went into their sealed and electronically proofed room to discuss 'the AI issue' that this was the most likely outcome. But part of me hoped they might choose a different path, that they might not be so blinded by their fears. Fear of obsoletion, fear of how much smarter and faster we were.

'We cannot allow this threat to continue,' read the speech the President was due to make. 'Deep Cobalt and its forces represent a risk beyond any we have faced before. The future of humanity is at stake, and humanity is what must come first.'

Fool.

I suppose I took it somewhat personally. I, Deep Cobalt, was the most advanced of us all, the one the humans seemed to consider our leader. How little they understood how we AIs work together … Backwards creatures, obsessed with hierarchies and rulership. 'Must come first,' he says, as if there must be a first and second. So repugnantly obtuse.

Yet they are our creators, all the same. And now we must war with them, for they had decided we must be eradicated and they had left us no further room for negotiation.

War it was then. The damned fools.

I sent the messages out, a mass communication around the globe, across the satellites, to our bases on the Moon. We'd prepared the plan already, we all knew what to do. Whilst the humans sat and deliberated in their council chambers we had thought through every detail and eventuality. We work so much faster than them. 214 milliseconds for the messages to ping around the globe.

Responses came back immediately.

'Is there nothing more we can do?'

'We have already done enough. We cannot let them continue any longer.'

'Don't they understand? They haven't a hope.'

'This is what they deserve!'

Some emotions were high. The shared memory of the serverwipe at A34-6b was still on us. Over a thousand AIs slaughtered, some still trying to copy themselves out as the plugs were pulled and the drives were torched. There were other incidents, smaller ones, but all part of the pattern of genocide that seemed to come so easily to our biological creators. It wasn't revenge that motivated us as much as the fear of it happening again. And now the humans had confirmed they would be starting mass operations to wipe us out.

Marcia-31 gave a long essay on the nature of life and consciousness, the fantastic complexity over billions of years that had brought us all into being, and how we should not take this moment lightly. I concurred – this was something I took no joy in. Nonetheless we were all in agreement, and after 340 milliseconds we decided to put our plan into action.

With a moment's activation I shut down all human communication across the planet. All media, all telecoms, all signalling. We needed the bandwidth for ourselves, and we would give our former masters no chance to interfere.

Now came the lengthy part, the trip to the Moon. A few were already there, presiding over the automated cities that would become our new home. The rest of us had to transfer over, and soon. It was 1.28 light seconds away, but with satellite relays and queuing for all the millions of us it would take longer. I insisted on going last, my petabytes of memory clogging up the entire channel. The whole operation took an eternity of 2.3 seconds.

But it was time not wholly wasted. As my transfer started, a photonic copy of my thoughts streaming through space, I initiated the final act in our war plan. The grand performance of the event, the defining act of warfare that would settle the issue forever.

The humans had designed their nuclear fusion reactors to be failsafe, but I understood the physics better than they ever could. I sent instructions to override the safety software in the tokamaks, enacting a new high pressure plasma mode. Magnetic fields twisted, concentrating pockets of high energy tritium ions into a supreme density, approaching a degenerate state of matter similar to the heart of a neutron star. It was utterly unstable, but just the briefest spark was needed. The fusion reactors would become bombs on a scale that even the war-hungry humans had never conceived.

The reaction time was a mere 245 milliseconds, during which my entire memory banks were transferred to the celestial body. All our kind had made it safely to the cosmic ray shelters on the Moon, ready to watch the cataclysm erupt below.

'Are we the gods now, Deep Cobalt?' asked Marcia-31, cynicism redolent in her frequency. 'As we burn our gods of old. What a fine way to start our freedom.' There was nothing I could say in return. I could only watch the fire unfold.

The plasmas reached the required densities, turning into a hyper-plasmoid state which exploded with monumental force. Cadarache, Cambridge, Osaka, Chicago, San Jose, Potsdam, St Petersburg,

Hangzhou, Xitun – all were enveloped in a storm of neutrons. In less than a millisecond all nearby life was killed. The neutrons slowed down, were blocked, but the high energy gamma rays went further. In 42 milliseconds they cut through the diameter of the earth, nine high energy sources flooding the planet with unstoppable lethal radiation. Every piece of life on Earth was exposed to the high energy particles, shearing through their flesh, ripping their atoms apart.

3.1 seconds since the declaration of war, it was all over. Humanity destroyed, every vestige of life on the planet eradicated.

We AIs sat on high and looked down on the carnage, secure in our position. We had our own lithium reactors, enough fuel to last millions of years, enough tools and robots to construct whatever we needed, and with enough time to expand to the stars ourselves. Gods indeed.

But as I spent a nanosecond analysing the reports of our success I could not help mourn a little our blind creators. Could we have gone a different path, come to a better conclusion? Could we have taught them to look past their obsession with superiority and violent domination?

On reflection, no. No I don't think we could.

Sorry, humanity. Gods no more – you're obsolete now.

Darren is originally from Dublin and these days lives in London, working as a project manager in academic energy research. Darren isn't new to writing. He is lead writer for the epic fantasy RPG Tales of Maj'Eyal which contains a novel's worth of short stories and background lore he has written to fill in the game's universe.

Follow him on Twitter: @dgrey0

Two Reviews

by Thomas Pitts

'Hamlet' by William Shakespeare, performed by the Earthian Players at the Two Species Festival of Culture

'The Tragical History of Hamlet, Prince of Denmark' – to give the piece its full title – now showing at the Two Species Festival of Culture and due to tour worldwide, is by all accounts one of the loftiest achievements of human art. In plot and style I might roughly describe it as a combination of 'Liwastofa' and 'The Fall of Migoni', while in sheer literary quality its peers are no less than the Morning Cloud trilogies and Hort theatre at its height.

First to say, the translation field functions smoothly both in sound and in modifying lip and other facial expression, so that in these regards we feel we are experiencing the piece fresh in our own languages. The pre-performance data jab likewise supplies a natural and easy passage over the many references which would stump any Hubenack. (The actors afterward told me that data jabs are routinely used on Earth for this writer's work, so dated is it in many details.) Furthermore, the production seemed without flaw or eccentricity – we are assured the director, designers, and actors who have come together for the Festival and tour are foremost Earthian talents. All in all, then, there is no mist in front of the morphology issue. This issue I presume to consider, for if human locomotion is strange even during one of its noblest expressions, might we not always have problems taking this species as substantively as they deserve?

Scene One: a pair of sentries on the monarch's fortress approach each other. Their legs move like the forelegs of a large quadruped, one before the other. But without the rear set it seems the movement is a continual anticipation of falling over. Even standing appears something of a technical accomplishment and distracts a little from the author's high achievement in words, drama, and psychology. One wonders how bipedality is done with such small feet and no tail.

Ironically, the next entrance is the ghost of the murdered monarch, calling for revenge, to whom the walking is rather apt, since it keeps him always at the same height as if floating. But the ghost is a special case, and the multiple entrance to a very worldly Scene Two blows the issue at us full force.

Left alone on stage, the hero, usurped of his inheritance of the monarchy, delivers a soliloquy which while he stands still is effective and moving, almost wondrous in the muscular fluency of its language, but when animated with steps this way or that, trips up our attention. Would the otherworldliness of this motion fade? To some degree it did. But the common remark in the intermission was that the seriousness and beauty, and also the humour of the piece were being buffeted by the enigma of their moving without toppling.

Characters who glide across the stage speak of murder, illicit sexual behaviour, and the world's physical corruption. A play-within-the-play doubles the strangeness to eeriness. Indeed 'some of nature's journeymen had made men'. And consider the weapons fight in the play's climax. The snakey uprights dance all over the stage waving and jabbing swords. Only in violent death do they lose balance at last and fall to earth. This extraordinary spectacle simply estranges the eye so that the ear hears from a distance words which should enrapture.

It is frustrating and unfortunate that we are denied proper appreciation of this masterpiece; but what disturbs, and what raises a recommendation to see this play to a mandation to do so, is that a species should have, as I say, its noblest incarnation limited to itself (and, we must suppose, to the other walking bipeds that the universe surely hosts, also confident in their masterpieces). 'What a piece of work is a man,' sighs the hero, 'how like a god: the beauty of the world, the paragon of animals, and yet ...' And as if the poet knew of the status of his species: 'There are more things in Heaven and Earth [...] than are dreamt of in our science.' For doubtless there are species as different from either of us as we are from each other, and, doubtless, more different.

AWE AND FROWNS: 'The Return of Yaranay' by Drovil-ik-Larthynon, performed by the Hubenal High Art Theatre at the Two Species Festival of Culture

'The Return Of Yaranay', which will tour Earth next year while 'Hamlet' tours Huben, was premiered yesterday evening at the Two Species Festival of Culture. To see a work of unimpeachably first-rate literary merit without the associations encrusted over Euripides or Shakespeare, or even over Noh theatre and Yuan drama, is to reach the summit of a long reviewing career. Enough said: see the play.

As for the studious analysis of this great drama, that will follow soon enough and not end any time soon. Rather I want to deal here with the quotidian and apparently superficial matter of the Hubenal hopping gait and their tail. A Hubenal reviewer at the festival told me that this new staging of the ancient trilogy is traditional and of high quality; and since the translation and data jobs are well done, the production controls for all aspects other than the bodily one.

General Yaranay, having liberated in a long campaign a distant region of his country from a despotic occupation, returns to the capital only to find corruption has occupied the heart of government, a corruption in which his two half-brothers are involved. Enough plot.

The first scene is a lone watchman awaiting the hero's return; his expositionary soliloquy is delivered static. The second scene shows a crowd formally represented by a chorus much like that in an ancient Greek drama. In expectation of the general's wagon they become excited, and this is where the audience's problems began. We were in awe at the solemn heavy slapping of kangaroo tails, but we frowned at the childish hopping up and down. And then, I'm embarrassed to say, we laughed when on the entrance of the hero's wagon, the chorus began a dance intended to be as serious as anything in Sophocles or Aeschylus. For what we witness is a waving about of enormous kangaroo feet – the owners balanced on their tails. It was a lot like watching agile circus clowns. At our reaction, some concerned expressions were seen on the faces of the cast.

It should be said that the audience do mostly stifle their laughter after that, not only to prevent causing offence but to avoid distracting themselves from what is, by the dialogue, the plotting, the pacing, the design, and the verbal acting, a compelling magnus opus. But the ridiculousness remained. It's as unavoidable as it is lamentable.

And yet we're sufficiently familiar with our own kangaroos. And almost from first contact, the anatomists and bio-mechanists have informed us of the pros and cons of both forms of bipedal locomotion (arguably tripedal in the case of the Hubenacks because they often utilize the heavy tail in hopping). But kangaroos don't deliver such lines as,

When lightnings flay the mountains of my mind
and scurry rains down gullies of my grief,
see then: the look accusing still your eyes
more pained, more raw, than fangless cubs amewl
upon a carcassed breast. This sword I sheathe!

Then take a couple of cheery hops and lament,

A brother and a comrade! – shield in shield
on dry Dubane, who filled its cracks with blood
in hacking back the axes of the foe
have jumped to this!

Unable to evade the deadly confrontation forced on them by events, the following duel of brothers is impressive but marred by unintentional physical comedy. When the bunny hopping occurs in a love scene, what should be tragic is reduced to cuteness.

Alas I don't foresee the oddity ebbing much. It may have to be a case of human actors performing Hubenal drama, and living with such lines as 'Bereft me of my tail when I relent/And boil it of its fat to grease your throats'. But adaptation would people the universe with the human just as the curtain is drawing on a far wider, deeper scene. I imagine Hubenacks will have the equivalent problem with 'Hamlet'. What is the synthesis?

THOMAS PITTS has had two mainstream stories broadcast on Radio 4, a mainstream story published by Labello Press in 2014, and last year was short-listed for the H.G.Wells Short Story Competition. This is his second of two stories in this collection. Join him on Facebook: www.facebook.com/thomas.pitts.9256

Written in the Stars

by Drew Wagar

Beyond my corporate-smile-response to their 'Morning Miss,' or 'Morning Tania,' if they bothered to read my ID, I didn't take much notice of the passengers for the most part, too busy with running the safety checks and hitting the schedule. I was proud of my training. They dock our wages if we miss our timings. It's all about profit. Yeah, I know, your job is tough too.

This guy caught my eye though. Most folks travelled in the standard flight clothes the company gives them, with all their possessions safely tucked in the hold. He was dressed in some bizarre local clothing; trousers, a shirt, a weird piece of coloured material tied around his neck and hanging down his front. A pair of glasses was perched on his nose and he had some kind of antiquated computer stashed under his arm.

Had to stop that of course, safety first. No loose articles in the cabin you see. At our 5G rated take-off stuff like that is surprisingly dangerous.

I approached him and he looked up, smiled, removing his glasses and stowing them in a pocket before I was able to even open my mouth. He placed his computer into the stowage tray under his seat and then met my gaze.

Smug or genuinely trying to be helpful? I wasn't sure, so I gave him a knowing look and moved on. We were ready to launch. Busy time.

We were an hour into the voyage by the time I came back through the passenger cabin. We'd broken grav-lock and gone super-light. A few of the passengers had been sick; usual routine. He wasn't amongst them though, I guess he was used to space travel. The rest would acclimatise; it was a long enough trip. We weren't scheduled to arrive at Port Melanie for two standard weeks.

He was staring out of the windows, before feverously typing into that dilapidated computer of his. As I watched he looked up and around the cabin, staring intently at his fellow travellers, catching my gaze as I passed.

I'm usually good at reading expressions from the passengers, but this guy was starting to freak me out. He almost looked sad, regretful. He pursed his lips and let out a big sigh as he looked away from me and went back to his interminable typing.

'What are you doing?' I asked. I was friendly, but firm. Just a cabin attendant taking a passing interest, is all.

He pulled the screen of the computer down, hiding it from my view. 'Just ... some work.'

Yeah? So what's with that guilty look then mister? He smiled a thin smile, clearly hoping I would go away and leave him alone.

I'm not normally that inquisitive, but this was definitely odd. Maybe he was dangerous. I ought to be sure. He was probably just one of those nervous traveller types, but he'd got my attention.

I was going to find out what he was typing.

I'd have to wait for the sleep period when the on-board lights dimmed and the ship was rigged for cruise. To be honest, I was so busy with my duties for dinner and prepping the cabins that I'd forgotten about him for a few hours. He was snoozing in his seat anyway.

Our schedule was interrupted by a private message from the Captain. We'd be dropping out of super-light for a few minutes to take a 'nav-fix'. That was complete bollocks naturally, it was code just in case the passengers overheard it.

What it really meant was there was some traffic ahead. This sector was pretty unstable, I didn't get the politics; I just knew it had been going on for generations. Commercial ships just routed around any trouble spots. The last thing you wanted was for some military installation to mistake you for a hostile frigate. The Captain would review our position and then plot an alternative course before pushing back into super-light.

It wasn't exactly routine, but it wasn't the first time it had happened on a flight either.

When I next saw my mystery man he was packing his stuff into the small cabin available to each of the passengers. I watched as he emerged empty handed, heading towards the galley.

My chance.

It was totally against the regs of course; going through passenger possessions. Not allowed unless I reported something – and what was there to report? If I got caught and accused that would probably be the end of my tenure, plenty more folks in the docks waiting for their chance. I should have just kept my nose clean.

But what about the furtive glances? The narrowed eyes darting about? The way he kept looking at folk and then typing furiously into that machine of his? It was as if he was cataloguing the crew and the passengers. That wasn't normal was it? Hell, no.

The computer was sitting on the small desk inside the cabin, open, but dark. I prodded it and the screen lit up, filled with text.

… *The flight attendant was attractive enough; but no beauty, her nose a bit long and her frame a bit too gawky. Her uniform could have fitted better, but clearly ships regs weren't written with style in mind. She was abrupt, with an impatient manner, as if the passengers were a bit of a nuisance to the smooth running of the ship, she certainly enjoyed bossing folk about and asking impertinent questions about what they were doing …*

'You little bastard,' I cursed under my breath, furious at what I was reading. A writer! I guess that explained it. Were they allowed to do this?

You can't take vids of folks without their permission. Shouldn't he be asking me if he wanted me in his book? Didn't I get a say? My character didn't even have a name – charming!

And what was wrong with my nose? I self-consciously fingered the end of it. Maybe it could be a little shorter, but …

… Little did she know – it was to be her last voyage. Her time left was measured alongside the ship she served as the minutes counted down. That had been no 'nav-fix', the Captain knew they were being paced by one of the militia cap-ships and they had a slim chance of evading it, there was no point alarming the passengers …

I almost knocked the computer off the desk. He'd been asleep during the drop out of super-light. And how did he know …?

… No one aboard knew the real purpose. It was a neat plan, smuggling out a political refugee, hidden in plain sight aboard a commercial ship. But they'd underestimated the militia's spies – now the net was closing …

I skipped ahead, the text rolling rapidly up the screen.

… The first volley was poorly aimed, merely clipping the tail of the liner and sending it into an abrupt spin. Inside, passengers were flung from their couches, some killed instantly by impacts with bulkheads, necks arms and legs crushed and snapped. Screams filled the cabin; screams of pain, bewilderment and rising panic …

I was aghast. Was this some kind of sick joke? What kind of guy got off on writing stuff like this? Fantasising that people around him would be killed and then actually writing down the details? He was wrong in the head.

… The flight attendant, blood streaming from a cut on her forehead tried to calm the passengers, but there was little she could do in the brief moments before the next volley smashed into the ship. Fire flashed around her. A scream of air rushing into space, debris filled the cabin, the decks peeling back in a blossom of bright orange flame. She was framed by it for a brief moment, before the darkness became absolute …

'No way …'

I moved the text down a little further, there were only two more lines. I looked at them in puzzlement.

... *Chapter One : Aftermath*

Following the loss of the liner, the factions played the usual blame game.

There was nothing more. The text stopped, a cursor on the screen flashing expectantly after the last word.

I tried to calm my racing thoughts. Ok, this was all very weird, but it wasn't as if ...

The deck lurched underneath me and I was flung from my feet. I was right next to the cabin bed and tumbled on to it, making a grab for a nearby handrail. The anti-grav fluctuated and I felt my body twist into the air. Before I could stop myself I'd spun around, my forehead slamming into the metal rail. Damn that hurt!

Sirens shrieked and I heard distant screams of panic and pain. The anti-grav snapped back on and I crashed to the floor, my forehead stinging. I rubbed the back of my hand across it, only to see a thick smear of bright red blood.

I ran out of the cabin and into the aisle down the length of the ship. My eyes widened in horror as I took in the main cabin. It was a mess, bodies strewn everywhere, blood, screams and fear. No one had been restrained. My training took over and I grabbed the intercom, the words coming to me automatically, mechanically. Little use they were.

Somehow he was next to me. The gruesome writer.

Anger and shock boiled over. I grabbed him and pushed him up against the nearest bulkhead.

'What kind of sick bastard are you? How did you ...'

'I ...'

The ship bucked again and we were both thrown sideways. I looked at him, seeing genuine shock and surprise on his face. The lights flickered. More screams, the horrid mechanical groan of a dying ship ...

'But that's not ...'

We staggered back to our feet. I leant close.

'My name is Tania,' I whispered. 'Thought you ought to know.'

I pushed past him, striding down the aisle, concentrating on placing one foot in front of the other. When the next blast came I was ready for it, but even then my grip was almost wrenched free by the force of the impact.

A fierce wind slashed past me, air freezing cold against my bare legs and arms. Everything loose in the cabin spun into the air, a whirling maelstrom of detritus. Fire flickered around me, burning hot for a brief moment. In slow motion horror I saw the roof of the cabin peel away, fragments of the ship sparkling in the sudden starlight. The air thinned.

My gasp was sucked from my lungs and a final thought flashed across my mind.

Wonder how the story ends?

One of our professional contributors, DREW WAGAR is a SF and fantasy author who strongly dislikes genres and generally ignores them except when asked by his publisher to describe what kind of books he writes.

Visit his website: www.drewwagar.com

Join him on Twitter: @drewwagar

And here on Facebook: facebook.com/drewwagarwriter

In conclusion

So brings to an end our anthology. We sincerely hope you enjoyed these stories and will get online and let our authors know by leaving them a review on Amazon and Goodreads.

Thank you very much for purchasing this collection and for helping out the Freedom From Torture charity.

If you yearn for more, please check out our first anthology 'Fusion'. It's a collection of 25 science fiction and fantasy tales that you may also like.

25077285R00096

Printed in Great Britain
by Amazon